FIRE BURN

FIRE BURN

Peter Turnbull

Severn House Large Print
London & New York

This first large print edition published 2008
in Great Britain and the USA by
SEVERN HOUSE PUBLISHERS of
9-15 High Street, Sutton, Surrey, SM1 1DF.
First world regular print edition published 2007 by
Severn House Publishers, London and New York.

British Library Cataloguing in Publication Data

Turnbull, Peter, 1950-
  Fire burn. - Large print ed. - (The Hennessey and Yellich
  series)
  1. Hennessey, George (Fictitious character) - Fiction
  2. Yellich, Somerled (Fictitious character) - Fiction
  3. Police - England - Yorkshire - Fiction 4. Detective and
  mystery stories 5. Large type books
  I. Title
  823.9'14[F]

  ISBN-13: 978-0-7278-7702-4

Printed and bound in Great Britain by
MPG Books Ltd, Bodmin, Cornwall.

One

Friday, December 12,
10.35 hours – 17.53 hours
in which a single murder becomes double.

It was some moments before the man realized that the thing, for this was the word that came to mind, the 'thing', was human. Or at least had, in life, been a human being. It did not at first look to be like anything the man had seen before, though he felt his eclipsed existence, as he saw it, acutely. A school leaver with no qualifications in a shrinking job market, he had eventually given up the search for employment and, by now, at the age of thirty-seven years, he had resigned himself to lifelong unemployment. He stayed at home except to sign for the dole Giro each week, watched television a great deal and occasionally, when sufficiently motivated, would go for a ramble in the semi-rural area near to where he lived. Thus, with his experience of life and the world being as limited as he felt it to be, he hesitated before accepting in himself that the thing he was looking at was indeed a corpse. It was small, he thought, small for a corpse, larger than child size but still small, blackened, charred...as if it had been burnt, no...no...he thought, more than burned, he had been burned once in his kitchen – he still had the scar. This was more than burning; there was a word, a word...he had heard it once or twice and there was a machine with the same name...burns cows when they get that disease, mad cow disease...they put the carcasses of a mad cow into one, flames licked all round it...he'd seen it on television.

Incinerated, that was the word...and the mad cow's carcass goes into an incinerator. This body looked like that: black and twisted out of shape, with the arms and legs raised up and the body shrunken, but bigger than a child's body. He looked about him, the sluggish river, the reed beds, black and leafless against a blue sky, the vapour trail of an airliner, high and distant. The grass underfoot was soggy, caused by frost melt. The same two logs were still there, the two logs that had been there as long as he could remember, the logs he had played on as a child, walking the length of one, jumping to the other and walking back...summer days when he and Tommy Davies talked about joining the army together, or other things they were going to do when they were 'grown up'. In the event Tommy Davies never got the chance to 'grow up', drowning in the river one hot, endless summer's day when he was thirteen or fourteen, whereas he had made it to adulthood but was destined not to become a soldier, or anything else. The only structure in his life from the age of sixteen to the present was the depressing, mechanical trudge to the dole office in York to sign on after the women stamped 'unemployed' seven times on his card. These women who had looked old when he first signed on 'until something turned up' and who now, over twenty years later, looked like young girls.

Here were the logs; two trees felled by a woodsman, probably before he and Tommy Davies were born, probably felled with the intention of moving them or reducing them where they lay, but which had, by accident or design, come to remain there for at least the whole of the man's life, probably longer.

Now there was a body lying between them, face up, grinning, it seemed, at the sky. The song birds sang, the magpies made their awful sound, the traffic hummed on the main road some quarter of a mile away, and beyond the road, a large goods train rumbled slowly, but steadily, along the railway track, the driver occasionally sounding the two-tone horn. The air, thought the man, had a clean, winter freshness about it, with a trace of mustiness rising from the ground and an all pervading smell of charred meat. To his right something rustled in the undergrowth, a squirrel he assumed, for such creatures had reached pest proportions of late. He had learned that from the television, for he spoke to few people and did not read the newspapers. The man turned from the body and began the slow walk back to the road and to the public phone box and to dial 999. He had only ever dialled 999 once before, after running near naked along the same path and in a panic after Tommy Davies had failed to surface.

He encountered a woman coming the other way before he reached the road. She was older than he, well dressed, her dog was a pedigree golden Labrador. She avoided eye contact as they closed with each other, looking past him, nervous of him or aloof, probably both, he couldn't tell, but he said, 'I wouldn't go down there, missus.' The woman walked on past him, ignoring him, until he added, 'There's a dead body,' at which she stopped in her tracks, as smartly as a serviceman coming to attention. She looked at him. 'By the logs,' he said. Then he asked, 'Do you have a mobile phone?'

George Hennessey looked down at the body, by then it, and the two logs, being enclosed in a large inflatable tent. He found himself mesmerized by the sight until the flash of SOCO's camera brought him back to the here and now, alerted him to the present.

'Male, female?' he asked.

'Police surgeon said, male, boss.' Yellich answered softly, in recognition of the reverence of the location. 'He took one look at the body, and said male, and pronounced life extinct at...' Yellich consulted his notebook. '11.10 this forenoon.'

'I see. I hope...hope he was dead before he was set on fire...for his sake. It's one of the deaths I fear.'

'Sir?'

'Being burned alive. I am not frightened of death, Yellich. It holds no fear for me...not in itself. The when of it does and the how of it does and this is one how I would be very pleased to avoid. The other is falling from a great height while conscious...So, I hope, for his sake, he was not alive when this was done to him.'

'Yes, sir, not a pleasant way to go.'

'Strange, don't you think?'

'Sir?'

'Well ponder...ponder if you will. There is no scorching of the logs or the ground...He wasn't set on fire here.'

'He wasn't, was he, sir? I see what you mean...he was carried here...like that.'

'Yes...a corpse is not a pleasant thing to

carry, well, I imagine not, but a charred corpse? I understand the flesh just comes off in your hand...like a well cooked joint, just falls apart...And it's been left where it was easily found...not concealed. Well, hardly concealed...hardly at all. Found by...?'

'A local man, sir. He was rambling, just to get out of the house for an hour or so.' Again Yellich consulted his notebook. 'Richard Boot by name. We have his address if you need to talk to him, but he didn't see anything. A lady walking her dog allowed him to use her mobile phone...and we are here.'

'And we are here.' Hennessey paused. 'You can even smell the burning...just...the odour is still detectable. He must have been dumped in the night. But why go to all that trouble? Why burn the man so completely...then carry him to where he will be easily found?' He glanced at Yellich.

'Beats me, sir. There's a river here. If they had put him in the river it would have been longer before he would be found, if ever, once the rats got their teeth into him...If they gnawed into the stomach, released the gasses, he'd sink, making a very tasty meal for fish, rodents and micro-organisms alike.'

'So they were not worried about him being found...just did not want him to be found in a location that would link him to the perpetrators.'

'Yes, sir.' Yellich smiled at Hennessey. 'That has to be the answer.'

'So, he won't be related to anyone who did this, nor a friend, nor a business partner... nor an enemy even.'

'Yes, sir, I see where you are going.'

'Into areas of great difficulty. This is possibly a gangland killing that will never be wrapped up. We'll likely identify him...then it will be a wall of silence. Nothing in the immediate area?'

'Constables are doing a fingertip search.'

'Yes, I saw...but no tracks that you noticed?'

'No, sir...the only footprints seemed to be of the man...Richard Boot and the lady dog walker. There was a frost last night, the ground would have been rock hard.'

'And the path leads to a road where a motor vehicle would have been parked, again without leaving any tyre tracks...and no houses close enough to be said to overlook the road where the path joins it?'

'No, boss...'

'Coming up against brick walls every way we turn, but let us not rush things. Somebody wanted this man dead, he had significance for someone...he meant something to somebody and at least some attempt was made to conceal the body, a token attempt, but an attempt. Didn't leave him on the side of the road for example...so whoever did this, didn't want an early discovery.'

The SOCO's camera flashed again.

'No, sir.'

'CCTV?'

'Not on this stretch of road, sir.'

Hennessey inclined his head. 'That would be too much to hope for, but then it might tell us something...it might imply local knowledge...Things are beginning to fall into place, Yellich.'

The curtain of the tent opened, a young and pale looking constable glanced at the charred remains as if unable to prevent himself from doing so and then looked at Hennessey. 'Dr D'Acre, sir.' He then stood back, holding the curtain, allowing Dr D'Acre to enter.

Dr D'Acre glanced at Hennessey and then

13

at Yellich. 'Gentlemen,' she said.

'Ma'am,' said Yellich. The SOCO remained reverentially silent.

'Doctor,' Hennessey murmured softly, 'one corpse of the male sex, pronounced life extinct by Dr Mann, the police surgeon, at 11.10 this day. Death appears suspicious.'

'I'll say!' Louise D'Acre looked at the corpse. 'He has assumed...his body has assumed the classic pugilistic pose of a person who when alive, or shortly after death, was burned. You see how the hands have risen up like a boxer defending himself?'

'Yes.' Hennessey spoke softly.

'Well, that wouldn't have happened to that degree if rigor had established itself. If rigor had established itself, the spine would have curved and contracted like a matchstick which is allowed to burn along its length, but the arms would have remained by his side. So if he wasn't burned to death, he was burned very shortly after he was life extinct ...within twenty-four hours. I am not going to take a rectal temperature; the thermal confusion caused by the incineration would make the exercise quite pointless. If you have finished here with photographs etcetera, you can have him transported to York District Hospital...I'll conduct the PM as soon as possible.'

'All finished?' Hennessey turned to the white overcoated Scenes of Crime Officer.

'All done, sir.' The man, portly and middle-aged, beamed as he recounted, 'Colour, black and white...all done.'

'Good.' Dr D'Acre allowed herself a brief smile, with lips coated with pale lipstick. 'Will you be observing for the police, Detective Chief Inspector?'

'Yes,' Hennessey said, nodding. 'Yes, I will.'

Again he saw the man. He glanced out of the window and took a moment's break and watched the man. He seemed to be elderly, but strode out like a youth, two fields distant, but the silver hair was clearly evident. He had noticed the man before, always at the same time, about eleven in the forenoon, walking the path through Denny Wood. He turned back to the room.

The charred corpse lay on the left of the

stainless steel table as viewed from Hennessey's vantage point at the side of the pathology laboratory. Hennessey was dressed in disposable green coveralls, as were Dr D'Acre and Eric Filey, the pathology assistant. Hennessey had encountered Eric Filey on a number of occasions whilst observing post-mortems for the police and had always found the youthful, rotund individual to be a cheery and warm personality; in complete contrast to all other pathology assistants he had met. All others, he had found, seemed to have let their work affect them; dealing with death, mortality, the essential frailty of the human body made them sour, humourless, cynical. Occasionally it had made them very fearful as in the case of one man Hennessey had met just once but who he remembered vividly because of the man's fear. This man had been a lowly assistant in a pathology laboratory for very nearly all his working life and then, in his sixties, knew that if there was anything even remotely suspicious about his death, then his corpse would be examined. He knew which laboratory in which hospital his body would be taken to, which table it would be lain on with a starched white towel covering his genitals, which of his colleagues would assist which pathologist, which tools would be used to dissect his body. When Hennessey met him, he was fearful of going out of doors, rarely ventured out at night and never alone, always being accompanied by his patient and very dutiful wife. But not so Eric Filey, late twenties, quiet unless spoken to, and then would reply with warmth. He was efficient too, good at his job, evinced by the respect he was always given by Dr D'Acre and other pathologists. At that moment he, like Hennessey, stood, knowing their place, waiting for comments or requests from Dr D'Acre.

Dr D'Acre stood beside the stainless steel table dressed, as Hennessey and Filey, in green disposable coveralls with a disposable hat and foot covers. She reached a slender arm upwards and adjusted an angle poise arm which was bolted to the ceiling, until the microphone on the lower end of the arm was just above her head and central to the table. The room was brilliantly illuminated by florescent bulbs that shimmered behind perspex sheets affixed to the ceiling.

17

'Unknown adult of the male sex.' Dr D'Acre spoke with received pronunciation in a clear voice, evidently for the benefit of the audio typist who would be handed the cassette tape at the conclusion of the post-mortem. 'Today's date, twelfth of December ...and give it a case number please.' She pondered the body. 'The body is covered with third degree burns, the deeper tissue below the skin is destroyed, subcutaneous fat and muscle tissue has been lost or severely damaged...this can be seen at a glance. The hair is almost completely burned away but sufficient survives to indicate that he had scalp hair above his ears and round the back of his head, but the scalp was probably bald...the skin is leathery to the touch.' Dr D'Acre took a scalpel and probed into the thigh. 'The soft tissue has been partially consumed by the fire...the bone itself is not blackened...the period of incineration was not very long and there may even have been an attempt to extinguish the flames. The burning is extensive to the point that all parts of the body are grossly affected. If this fire had been left to run its course, the body would eventually have cremated, leaving only bones and internal organs. This fire was either extinguished...or...it took place in an enclosed space and the flames consumed all the oxygen and the fire expired before cremation occurred. There are a number of splits to the skin which seem similar to knife wounds but are in fact consistent with burning...They are where we would expect to find such splitting, the elbows and knees and they show no bleeding...so safely fire damage. I can detect no sign of antemortem injury –' she glanced at Hennessey – 'but the day is young. I think we all want to know whether this gentleman was mercifully deceased before he was incinerated...so let's find out.'

Dr D'Acre took a scalpel from the tray and drove an incision into the larynx of the corpse and opened the incision. 'Well, what we are looking for is soot deposits below the vocal chords...soot can enter the mouth of a corpse but it cannot pass beyond the vocal chords unless the person is breathing and here...here, you will both be relieved to note that there is no soot in the lower respiratory tract, so fortunately for this man, he did not die as a result of the fire. He was deceased before he was set alight...Rather rules out my suggestion that someone tried to put out the fire and lends weight to the corpse being burned in an enclosed space which had a finite supply of oxygen. Foul play, rather than an accident...at least it points that way. So, if the fire didn't kill him, what did? Well, there is no sign of trauma over and above the fire-damaged tissue so we have to dig deeper...So let us first look at his skull.'

Again Dr D'Acre took the scalpel and drove an incision round the head, just above the ears. She then laid the scalpel in the tray at the foot of the table and with slender, latex-encased hands and fingers, removed the skin from the top of the skull. 'Just out of the oven,' she remarked with, what Hennessey thought, to be uncharacteristically dark humour. 'This fire didn't take place a long time ago, but that observation has been made earlier. The ease with which the skin peels from the bone serves to confirm it.' She laid the fold of charred and brittle skin beside the skull. 'Ah...and here we have the cause of death...well, a probable cause of death...massive fracturing of the skull...

radial fractures like spokes of a wheel radiating from a central point. A flat surface... falling headfirst on to concrete would have caused injuries like this, in the case of an accident, or a spade in the case of intentional injury...something flat and hard...This injury would have killed him outright. A single, forceful blow to the top of his head...the...blood hasn't cavitated.'

'Cavitated?' Hennessey repeated.

'Yes, in cases of burning of human bodies ...and animal...the blood boils and is forced by the heat into the cavity between the brain and the skull. It doesn't look like blood by then, more like thick green soup, but that hasn't happened and that further indicates that the fire, while consuming his body, didn't last long. It seems to me that the fire was an attempt to conceal his identity. They may have thought that they had succeeded and contented themselves with what they had achieved rather than wanting to reduce the body further...no clothing...no trace of fabric...no zip fasteners melted to the body, no trace of leather or rubber on the feet...no wristwatch...all removed. He wouldn't have done that by himself in the winter...no naturist here...His clothing was removed and why? Well, that is your department, Detective Chief Inspector. I do not wish to intrude.'

'Oh, intrude all you like, ma'am.' Hennessey raised his voice slightly to allow it to carry across the laboratory. 'All help gratefully received, but I take your point, identity concealment seems to be emerging as an issue in this case.'

'Well...let's help you all we can. Mr Filey...if you could help me?'

Hennessey watched as Eric Filey and Dr D'Acre, with seeming ease, rolled the charred corpse on to its side. Dr D'Acre then took a tape measure and laid it the length of the spine. 'Two feet eight inches,' she said, 'or approximately eighty-one centimetres. That would make him about five feet four inches tall, but the fire would have caused some shrinking, probably by as much as two inches. So, he would have been about five feet six inches in height or one metre and sixty-seven centimetres in European newspeak. I can get a better idea of his height once I measure the femur and tibia and other long bones and from them deduce the height of the gentleman, but five foot six is a close approximation, the spine being half the overall height of a normally proportioned person and this gentleman appears normally proportioned. Fashion models with endless legs tend to upset that theory but, lucky them, they are not normally proportioned. So...if we can roll him back, please, Mr Filey?'

Again Hennessey watched the skill and apparent ease with which the corpse was turned gently over on to its posterior.

'We'll look at the mouth...a veritable gold mine of information.' Dr D'Acre took a length of stainless steel and forced it between the teeth and then prised the mouth open, causing a distinct 'crack' to the head as the rigor was broken. 'Well, he's Northern European...or Caucasian...the teeth tell us that and he has had recent dental work...and British dentistry...so his identity will be easy to confirm once you have a name and someone to tell you who his dentist was. Dentists are obliged to keep their records for eleven years, but this dental work appears to be quite recent...within two or three years I'd say...the fillings are not

23

decayed. I'll extract one of his teeth, send it to the forensic science laboratory at Wetherby, they'll cut it in cross section and that will give them his age to within twelve months. So let's see what he had for his last meal. Better take a deep breath, gentlemen...' Dr D'Acre once again took the scalpel and drove an incision across the stomach allowing intestinal gases to escape with a loud 'hiss'.

'Smelled worse,' she said, 'and the presence of gas is further indication that the fire was of brief duration. The gases not smelling as strongly as they otherwise might means that this gentleman is recently deceased. This is not the case of a three-, four-day-old corpse being set alight and then dumped; this gentleman was set alight soon after losing his life...and within the last twenty-four hours. He also ate shortly before he died...a substantial meal... which is still discernible...chicken, I think...yes...and vegetables, rice...peas...mushrooms...chicken curry. This man did not know he was going to die, he enjoyed a chicken curry and then met his end.'

Dr D'Acre stepped sideways towards the

head. 'The facial features are unrecogniz-
able and seem to have suffered more damage than the rest of the corpse...It's as if
the accelerant was poured over the face to
attempt to disguise, or even destroy the
features, and flames spread out from there.
I wouldn't say that this was a random attack
– as you have said, Mr Hennessey, attempt-
ed concealment of identity is an issue here –
but this is not gangland, it's too messy, too
careless in my experience, and I dare say
in yours. There is panic here; there is an
absence of knowledge of forensic proce-
dures...facial reconstruction now takes a
matter of seconds with digital imaging. All
the computer operator needs is an X-ray of
the skull and an image can be conjured on
the screen within seconds. Used to take
weeks building the face up using plasticine
on the actual skull, but the depth of tissue is
in the computer program; all the operator
needs is the sex, race and age.'

'All of which you have kindly provided.'

'Except the age; Wetherby will give you
that once I give them a tooth. We'll X-ray
the skull before I extract the tooth...send
the X-ray to Wetherby along with the tooth.

So, adult, West European male, well nourished, addressed dental hygiene, was killed by a massive blow to the skull which may or may not have been deliberate...but then there followed a clumsy and as I said, apparently panic-driven attempt to conceal the identity of the person in question, and by someone not of the criminal fraternity. A criminal would not panic and would know of forensic techniques. The body was probably burned inside an enclosed space that was not combustible – a metal container, for example. There is no sign of clothing on the body. The fire was of brief duration and had he been clothed, some remnants of fibre would be present. Similarly, there is no metal as from zip fasteners or a watch etcetera...similarly no footwear...Again points to an attempt to conceal his identity.' She paused. 'I'll trawl for poisons as a matter of course, but I feel in my waters it will be futile, the massive fracturing of the skull seems to be the cause of death, as if someone crept up behind him and whacked him over the head with a spade, then panicked. So, over to you, Mr Hennessey, my report will be with you tomorrow, but that is the nuts and bolts...over to you.'

'Over to me.' George Hennessey halted just inside the door of the hospital and braced himself to meet the blast of cold air that was the wind, a bitter north-easterly that drove across the city of York and the surrounding area. He screwed his fedora down round his head, buttoned up his overcoat and turned up his collar. Then he stepped purposely out of the centrally-heated cocoon that was the hospital. He strode down Gilleygate and instead of joining the walls as was his usual custom, knowing like every York resident that by far the speediest way to cross the centre of the city is to walk the walls, he chose to walk up Micklegate, believing the walls would be too exposed. 'Over to me.' Dr D'Acre's words rang in his ears. He thought of the victim, a male who ate well, and who cared for his teeth...such a man would be integrated...such a man would be missed...soon someone will be weeping.

He entered the main entrance of Micklegate Bar police station, nodded in response to the duty constable's deferential greeting of 'Good afternoon, sir', and opened the

'Staff Only' door and closed it behind him. He signed as being 'in' and checked his pigeonhole. There was nothing of importance, he thought: the usual reminder about saving money by writing on both sides of a sheet of paper, and notification of a retirement party for an officer he only vaguely knew. Such notices of retirement parties once held little significance for him but now he was silver haired and with liver-spotted hands...soon...very soon, the staff in the division would be plunging their hands into their pigeonholes and extracting a notice of a retirement party for DCI George Hennessey of Micklegate Bar police station. But not, he thought, not for a few months yet, a good few months at that. Time enough, he thought, time enough to crack the case of the charred corpse and a few more cases after that.

He walked on to his office, noticing that Yellich was not at his desk as he passed his office. In his own office he peeled off his overcoat and hung it on the coat stand, putting his hat on the peg above his coat. He kept his jacket on, the police station not, he found, being as generously heated as was

York District Hospital. He then picked up the phone on his desk and made two internal phone calls, the first to the collator asking for any recent missing person reports involving adult Caucasian males of about five and a half feet or one metre sixty-seven centimetres in height; the second call was to the press officer, and between them they created, word by word, a press release. It was done, advised the press officer, in sufficient time to be included in the early evening news bulletins of the regional television networks, and for the final edition of the evening paper. The local radio stations would be carrying the story on their hourly news broadcasts. He thanked the press officer and replaced the handset of his phone gently as his eye was caught by a solitary figure walking the walls, hunched forwards, in a blue duffel coat. Hennessey watched the man until he was obscured from view by the confines of the small windows of Hennessey's office. He then turned his attention to the task in hand, phoned the collator again, asked for a crime number and was given 12/161. He noted the number on his notepad along with the date, and ruminated that already, by the twelfth of December, there had been 161 crimes reported in York Division alone. Most, he knew, would be petty and non-violent and 12/161 would be the first murder, perhaps even the first serious offence. York, after all, is a seat of learning, a seat of justice and a cathedral city; it attracts tourists but it does have a rough underside on Friday and Saturday nights when the agricultural labourers and the coal miners come in from small towns in the Vale wanting their beer, women and fights. Despite that, 12/161 would be the first murder.

Case number 12/161 would also be unlike most murders which are products of fights in pubs or domestic disputes, where the death of the victim was not necessarily intentional, where witnesses often abound, and where the identity of the victim is known from the outset. Here the victim's death appeared intentional; here efforts to hide the victim's identity had been made, clumsily so, but made nonetheless. Further, this murder was, as Dr D'Acre pointed out, unlikely to be gangland; it was too messy. That, pondered Hennessey, would equally both help and hinder the police. Gangland would know how to cover their tracks, the perpetrators of this murder did not; that would prove to be useful, but gangland members are known to the police. It is a rite of passage that every gangland member must have done prison time, and prison time means a police record, it means finger-prints and possibly DNA on file; all good assistance to any police investigation. The perpetrators of this crime, however, might be Mr and Mrs Clean; no flies on them at all.

He sat back, causing his chair to creak. There was more than one perpetrator, if only because it would have taken more than one person to carry the corpse to where it was found. Two men minimum could have done it but he had a feeling that more than two were involved. Having seen the crime scene, having viewed the body wedged grotesquely between two tree trunks, he felt it likely to have been a job undertaken by three or four persons. A conspiracy; and that would also equally both help or hinder the police. If the conspirators held firm, maintained a wall of silence, then the police would have an uphill task, but should one of the conspirators lose their nerve, or be tempted to talk by inducement of the promise of lesser charges being levelled, then... then the conspiracy is doomed. We shall see, said Hennessey to himself, what we shall see.

There was a tap on the frame of his office doorway. DS Yellich stood there, wrapped in an overcoat. Hennessey smiled at him. 'Come in, Yellich.'

'Thanks, skipper.' Yellich walked into Hennessey's office and sat on a chair in front of Hennessey's desk. 'Not a great deal to report, I'm afraid.'

'Oh...? Tea?'

'Yes, please.' Yellich rubbed his hands. 'That wind is a biter...not so cold out of the wind but...what's that term? Chill factor? The chill factor is high...time to dig out the thermals, methinks.'

'Methinks too...' Hennessey stood and walked to the corner of his office where a kettle, milk, teabags and half a dozen mugs stood upon a small table. He checked that the kettle contained sufficient water and then switched it on. 'So, anything at all?' He poured milk into two mugs.

'No, sir...fingertip search of the area proved negative...nothing to show for a lot of constables with numb fingertips. The gentleman who found the body was eager to help but more out of a need for human company, poor soul. Lives alone, never worked in his life, not a single day's work since leaving school. Didn't seem to be the employment-avoiding type, just no luck, but he couldn't tell us anything.'

'Well, I've contacted the press officer and the collator. Dr D'Acre confirms that he was dead before being set on fire; death was caused by a massive blow to the head. You don't take sugar, do you?'

'No, thanks, skipper.'

Hennessey placed a teabag in two mugs and added boiling water. 'Wetherby will come back with an age tomorrow once they have extracted a tooth, and Dr D'Acre will supply an X-ray of the skull.'

'Facial reconstruction?'

'Yes. One tea.' Hennessey handed Yellich one of the mugs. The other he carried with him as he returned to his chair.

'Cheers.' Yellich grasped the mug of hot

liquid with two hands. 'So, if the fire wasn't the cause of death, then someone wants to conceal the person's identity.'

'Yes...I was pondering the same just a moment ago. Dr D'Acre was able to find indications that the fire was starved of oxygen, as if the fire was contained within a small space, like a metal container...something like that. And more than one perpetrator.'

'Yes...I thought two at least to be able to carry the corpse from the road to where—'

The phone on Hennessey's desk rang. He let it ring twice before picking it up. 'DCI Hennessey.'

Yellich watched as colour seemed to drain from Hennessey's face, and his jaw seemed to drop. Hennessey scribbled on his notepad.

'Thank you...got that.' Hennessey spoke softly. He replaced the handset gently on to the rest and glanced at Yellich. 'We've got another one...another charred corpse. Opposite side of the city, out by Heslington Common.'

Yellich gulped his tea. 'Other side of York, as you say, boss, but has to be linked.'

34

'Oh, yes.' Hennessey drank his tea in mouthfuls. 'Can't be a coincidence. Well... we're wanted...no rest for the wicked.'

Yellich drove. The distance from Micklegate Bar police station to Heslington Common was short, just a ten-minute drive. Following directions, they arrived efficiently at the scene, the blue flashing lights of the police cars against a drab background providing a clear homing beacon on the last stage of the journey. They left the car and walked together, with Yellich a half step behind Hennessey, to where a blue and white police tape, tied to trees, had cordoned off a small area of ground within a stand of small trees and shrubs. Four constables and a sergeant stood by the tape; a turban-wearing man knelt within the confines of the tape. The trees swayed. Hennessey held on to his fedora, Yellich's coat collar butted his jaw. The sky had turned overcast.

As Hennessey and Yellich approached, the turban-wearing man stood and then bowed under the tape and stood again. He nodded at Hennessey and Yellich. 'Good day,' he said reverently with a faultless English accent.

'Good day, Dr Mann,' Hennessey replied. He glanced beyond the tape where he could see blackened limbs rising from the tall grass. 'Another charred corpse, I understand.'

'Indeed yes, of the female sex on this occasion. I have just arrived, summoned by the constables, and will confirm life extinct at...' Dr Mann glanced at his watch. '4.47 p.m....16.47 hours this day.'

'16.47 agreed,' Hennessey replied. Out of the corner of his eye he saw Yellich retrieve his notebook from his pocket and begin to take notes.

'The body is that of an adult female... charred...incompletely burned...no destruction of the skeleton...again, as was the case this morning.'

'I see. Well, thank you, sir.' Hennessey again glanced towards the charred corpse.

'I will take my leave now. I will forward my report to you forthwith.'

'Thank you, sir.'

Dr Mann inclined his head and walked away towards his car, carrying his black bag with him.

'Found by?' Hennessey turned and addressed the uniformed sergeant.

'Children, sir.'

'Children! At this time?'

'Truants, sir. They were quite shaken. I think they'll be in school next week.' The sergeant forced a smile, not inappropriately, thought Hennessey. 'Seems they realized that they can either make the most of their educational opportunities or they can find dead bodies. The former seemed to be the more attractive to them now. They were quite young...twelve, thirteen, four of them. They were on their way home after spending the afternoon on the common...saw the body...ran the rest of the way. Saw a police vehicle parked by the roadside and reported it to the constable. The constable investigated and called it in. Myself and the other constable were in the vicinity, we were diverted to assist. I called SOCO, the police surgeon and CID. Scenes of Crime Officers are yet to...ah...' The sergeant glanced beyond Hennessey. 'Just arriving now, sir.' Hennessey turned and saw a white van with SOCO in large black letters on the side, approach the parked police vehicles.

'Alright.' Hennessey stepped forward.

'Let's have a look before they get to work with their cameras.'

The sergeant lifted the blue and white tape to allow Hennessey and Yellich to ingress the cordoned off area. The two CID officers stopped short of the corpse at a point where they had a sufficiently full and clear view. It was as Dr Mann had described: a corpse, clearly female, lying face up with arms and legs raised in the pugilistic posture of a burned corpse. It was completely blackened, facial features were indistinguishable, the scalp hair had been destroyed and again, so far as Hennessey could tell, after learning from Dr D'Acre's observations of earlier that day, there appeared to be no clothing upon the corpse, no remnants of fabric, no metal, no trace of footwear.

'Damn strange,' Hennessey muttered.

'Sir?'

'Well, why leave them so far apart, yet so easily discoverable? This corpse is marginally more concealed than the male corpse but only marginally, it would have been found easily enough...if not today, then tomorrow; the common is very popular with dog walkers and folk just out for a walk to clear the tubes. So why not just leave the two bodies together somewhere?'

'Strange, as you say, sir.'

'"Fire burn and cauldron bubble. Fire burn and cauldron bubble",' Hennessey mumbled, almost to himself. 'Well,' he said, louder now, 'we'd better let the SOCO crack on. Can you please contact Dr D'Acre... apologize, but ask her to attend.'

'Yes, of course.'

'Then return to the station and ask the press officer to modify the press release, not one, but two charred corpses. In the name of the Creator I hope there won't be any more...two is sufficient. I'll remain here.'

It was Friday, 17.53 hours.

Two

Saturday, December 13,
9.27 hours – 23.10 hours
*in which a successful marriage is explored and
both George Hennessey and Somerled Yellich
are at home to the gracious reader.*

Hennessey reclined in his chair and read the reports. Dr D'Acre's report on the male victim contained no new information; it was rather a confirmation of the findings of the post-mortem: death was caused by a massive blow to the skull; the fire damage was post-mortem; a trawl for poison as a matter of course had proved negative. Dr D'Acre had toiled into the previous mid-evening to complete the post-mortem on the female victim, with George Hennessey once again observing for the police, and he was more

41

than impressed to have received her report by 09.15 on the Saturday. She must have dictated it to the secretary at 8.30 a.m. and had it sent to him by courier. Again, the report added nothing to the findings of the previous evening: the victim was female, Western European, also had had British dental treatment. Her larynx was crushed, minor bones in her neck had been broken; she had been strangled. Like the male victim, she too had also eaten a curry just before she had been murdered. Interestingly, her fingernails, which had survived the fire, showed no sign of damage which would normally have been expected; 'So-called defence injuries,' she reported, 'are not present which,' she concluded, 'means that sadly there is no trace of her attacker's blood beneath her fingernails and hence no DNA to be obtained.' Dr D'Acre concluded that the absence of defence injuries suggested the victim was restrained in some way, or was perhaps unconscious. The report from the forensic science laboratory at Wetherby stated that the tooth from the male victim indicated his age to be fifty-seven years, plus or minus twelve months.

An X-ray of the male victim, the reported added, was being 'worked up' to provide a digital facial reconstruction.

Hennessey stood and took the reports to Yellich's office. 'Busy?'

'The hit-and-run, sir.' Yellich looked up from the report that he was writing.

'Oh, yes.'

'Seventeen years old...everything to live for, now she's going to spend the rest of her life in a wheelchair.'

'Knocked off her bike, wasn't she?'

'Yes, sir...last Wednesday. No witnesses but the vehicle will have been damaged. We're talking to all the local garages; somebody will have been approached with a repair job to the front near-side bumper. What have you there, more work for I?'

'Reports from Dr D'Acre and Wetherby.'

'Already?'

'Yes, efficient is not the word.' Hennessey handed the reports to him and sat in the chair in front of Yellich's desk while Yellich read them.

'Husband and wife, do you think?' Yellich put the reports down on his desk.

'Probably. We haven't heard from Wetherby yet about the age of the female victim, but that's what I was thinking...a husband and wife ...out for a curry on Friday night, not expecting any bad news and a few hours later, they are no longer with us and their flesh is cooked.'

'No indication of clothing on the female victim?'

'None...but look at Dr D'Acre's report on the female victim...notice anything? I mean in comparison to the male?'

Yellich held up the two reports side by side and glanced at one, then the other. 'Good Lord!'

'Yes,' Hennessey said and smiled. 'She towered over him. He was five foot six or thereabouts and she, statuesque goddess, was over six feet tall. They would have made a striking couple.'

'I'll say. So is this for me, legwork for the Detective Sergeant? Visit all the Indian restaurants in York?'

Hennessey shrugged. 'You can do if you feel in need of the exercise but...you know Napoleon Bonaparte?'

'Heard of him. We did British history at school.'

'Well, he conquered half of Europe and you know the two qualities he looked for in his generals?'

'Tell me.'

'Intelligence and laziness.'

'Really?' Yellich smiled.

'Well, my collection of military history is not immodest, as you know, and I have read such. He had no time for intelligent and hardworking generals; he reasoned that if someone was hardworking and intelligent then he was stupid.'

'Cynical.'

'Probably...nay certainly...but, like I said, this fella very nearly achieved what the European Community is only now beginning to achieve. You see, he thought that if the hardworking general was ordered to take the army to the other side of the mountain he would take it over the top...up one side and down the other.'

'Fair enough.'

'But the lazy and intelligent general would do no such thing. Being intelligent, he would realize that he had to come up with the goods if he wished to keep his generalship, but being lazy he would find the easiest way to achieve that end, and so he'd take his army round the side of the mountain. Get to the same place with much less effort and that is in the interest of the army as a whole. Laziness and intelligence; believe me, that is a devastating combination of traits in any man.'

'Ah, I see where you are going, skipper. I can tramp round the city or I can use the phone.' Yellich smiled.

'Exactly. I'd leave it for an hour or so; they won't be open for business until lunchtime, but the managers will be at their desks by about ten. If you get a result, I'll be in my office.'

'Yes, boss.' Yellich made a long arm for the Yellow Pages that lay at the far corner of his desk.

Hennessey returned to his office, and with some reluctance, but also knowing the importance of same, he began to address his paperwork. Monthly statistical returns for November had to be concluded by the end of the following week; overtime claims for junior officers had to be approved; a reference for an officer who wanted to transfer to another part of the UK for personal reasons

– Stoke-on-Trent, a godforsaken, soulless, nothing of a place in Hennessey's view, but his fiancée wouldn't leave her home town, so the cheery constable had explained. Hennessey thought the young man deserved a good reference and Hennessey would find pleasure in writing it.

He had concluded the reference and put it in his out tray for onward conveyance to the typing pool where the secretaries, equipped with state-of-the-art word processors, worked and typed, but which was still called the typing pool, when Yellich tapped on the door frame of his office.

'Got a result,' he said with a smile.

The Last Viceroy restaurant stood in Gillygate between two terraced houses.

'Wouldn't want to live there,' Yellich observed as he and Hennessey walked to the door of the restaurant.

'Oh?'

'Too near an eatery. Had a friend once... when he was renting before he bought his first house, had a flat above a Chinese restaurant. He spent a fortune on food and ballooned, just never stopped eating – the continuous smell of food from the restaurant, you see, made him feel constantly hungry. Something me and Sara bore in mind when we were looking for a flat when we were first married.' He pressed the doorbell.

'It may be them.' The proprietor was Asian, in his early thirties, but spoke with a solid Yorkshire accent. Second, third, even fourth generation migrant, thought Hennessey. He seemed keen to help the police. 'It is the description...tall woman and short husband...it is sometimes seen, usually the other way round. My sister will only go out with men who are taller than her. So the description did ring a bell...if it's them.'

'They being?'

'Mr and Mrs Dent. They are regular customers. They don't come into York to eat but often eat at the end of their working day before going home. We have been open for three years and they have been regular customers from the day we opened. They are both accountants; they gave me some advice once which saved me a lot of money but I can't say I am their client. I did ask if they would take my account but they declined, most politely, but declined nonetheless. They didn't want to mix business with pleasure. So they explained.'

Hennessey glanced about him. The restaurant was decorated with embossed wallpaper in a rich scarlet colour, with prints of India, the Taj Mahal, the Gateway of India; a portrait of Earl Mountbatten, the Last Viceroy, hung by the door to the kitchen from which clattering sounds and the smell of Indian meals emanated. The table at which they sat had a starched white linen tablecloth and neatly folded paper napkins.

'How old are they?' asked Hennessey.

'Fifties, I'd say. As Mr Yellich asked, the age is correct.'

'Where do they live?'

'I'm afraid I don't know except that it is in the Vale, a car drive from the city.'

'Where are their business premises?'

'Precenters Court, by the Minster.'

'Yes, I know where it is. Posh address.'

'Doesn't get posher.' The man, Ali Kahn by name, smiled.

'And they ate here last night?'

'Thursday, boss,' Yellich corrected.

'Yes, sorry, last Thursday evening.'

'Yes...definitely...two nights ago. Chicken

Korma...neither of them like hot curry.'

'When was that?'

'Early to mid evening...they probably arrived at 6.00 p.m., waited to be served...we knew that...happy to let the rush hour die down. So they ate from 7.00 p.m. until about 8.00 p.m....didn't drink, a pitcher of chilled water between them...again, that was usual.'

'How did they seem?'

'Seem?'

'Their manner...attitude?'

'Oh...quite normal. They didn't look particularly happy as though they'd come into big money...nor did they look particularly upset...just a couple. They always looked very happy together...Very calm and content in each other's company...a settled marriage. I envy them. Why the police interest in them, may I ask? They are a very proper couple.'

'We...well...' Hennessey paused. 'Let's just say that we think they can help us with our inquiries and we are sure they are a very proper couple, as you say.'

'Well, the people you should talk to are their employees in Precenters Court. Can't miss their door, Dent and Dent, Chartered Accountants.'

It was just a five minute walk from The Last Viceroy on Gilleygate to Precenters Court, but the two streets were a world apart. Busy, bustling Gilleygate of small shops and houses and Precenters Court, a quiet cul-de-sac of Georgian terrace houses just on one side of the road, facing the high brick wall that was the boundary of the grounds of York Minster. Dent and Dent, Chartered Accountants was easily found. An imposing black gloss painted door which had to Hennessey a warm feeling, despite the colour being associated with mourning and tragedy. The office lights were on, a secretary could be seen tapping on to a keyboard of a word processor. Hennessey tried the door. It was locked. He pressed the buzzer attached to the 'squawk' box set in the wall.

'Hello?' The voice was soft, female, welcoming. 'Do you have an appointment?'

'We'd like to see Mr and Mrs Dent.'

'Well, I'm afraid you need an appointment.'

'It's the police.'

'Oh...please wait.'

Hennessey and Yellich waited. The door was opened within a few seconds by a middle-aged man in a woollen suit.

'Mr Dent?'

'No. You are the police?'

'Yes. Is Mr Dent in?'

'No, Mr and Mrs Dent don't work on Saturdays, neither do we normally but we have a backlog to clear.'

'I see. Where might we find Mr Dent...and Mrs Dent as well?'

'Why, is there some trouble?' The man was slightly built, well dressed, and seemed to both Hennessey and Yellich to be very serious minded.

'Yes, in a word,' Hennessey replied, craning his neck to look up at the man who stood on the elevated step of the doorway of the building. 'Might we come in?'

'Well...yes...yes.' The man stepped aside and allowed Hennessey and Yellich to enter.

'Very impressive.' Hennessey swept his hat off as he entered the hallway, high ceilings, complex plaster cornices, a large chandelier, deep pile carpets, polished hardwood furniture.

'Yes...it's a lovely old building, Regency or late third Georgian, I believe. Must have been a lovely family home but now these buildings are too large for single family occupancy. I mean, who could afford all the servants?' the man said with a humour which Hennessey didn't expect to see. 'Masson.'

'Sorry?'

'Masson. My name is Bernard Masson, chartered accountant, but employed, not a partner.'

'So I gathered,' Hennessey said, smiling, 'otherwise the brass plaque would be Dent, Dent and Masson, I assume.'

'Yes...a partnership would be pleasant, so would one's own practice, but employee status has its compensations...security and peace of mind. Anyway, shall we go to my office?' Masson shut the heavy front door behind him and walked past Hennessey and Yellich, leading them down the long corridor. 'Very York,' Masson said as he walked with a purposeful stride.

'Sorry?' Hennessey followed in Masson's wake.

'Very York...this building...old York at

53

least, narrow frontage, but the building goes back a long way, very deep. Frontage of about twenty feet...but forty or fifty feet from front to back, very York.'

'As you say. Any cellars?'

'Oh, yes...extensive cellarage, of course, but we are prone to flooding.'

'I thought you might be.'

'So we can't use them. The Minster is just on the other side of the wall, as you know, and a few years ago the Bishop of York rowed a small boat up the aisle of the Minster to the nave...famous photograph of that event.'

'I seem to recall seeing it.'

'Well, with that level of flooding occurring once every four or five years, we can't use the cellar, except perhaps for storage of non valuable, non perishable items but that's all...such a pity not to be able to utilize all that space.' He turned into a room. 'Please take a seat.' He indicated a row of armchairs in front of his desk. 'We do like to ensure client comfort as well as satisfaction,' he explained, as if seeing the expression of surprise on his visitors' faces.

'Dare say that keeps you in business.'

Hennessey sank into one of the armchairs. Yellich followed suit.

'Well, that's the name of the game, as in all businesses; a satisfied customer will return with more work.' He sat behind his desk, leaning back in a hinged, high back, blue executive chair. The window behind him looked out on to a small garden with a high brick wall beyond which were seen the backs and roofs of the houses of High Petergate. 'How can I help you?'

'By describing Mr and Mrs Dent.'

'Describing them?'

'Yes.'

'Well...both C.A.s, built up this partnership over twenty-five years, live quietly...out by Malton way.'

'Their appearance?'

'Appearance? That is a strange question.'

'If you'd answer it.'

'Well, Mr Dent, Anthony, he is a man of modest size in terms of height...smaller... shorter than myself. I am five feet eight inches. I still think in Imperial measurement, so Tony would be about five six I should think. Muriel, that is Mrs Dent, is a statuesque six foot plus. I look up to her, down to him...literally. I mean, not in any other way; they both have my respect as individuals and professionals in what can be a stressful occupation at times.'

'I know what you mean. Do you have their address?'

'West End House, Great Sheldwich... that's in the Vale of York, off the Malton Road, the A64.'

'Yes.'

'Well, follow the A64 as far as High Hutton, turn right, you'll come to Low Hutton, turn left there...well, you have to because the road doubles back to the A64, but Great Sheldwich is just after Low Hutton.'

'You've been there?'

'Does it show? Yes, the Dents are very hospitable, have an annual dinner party for the staff each summer...lay on taxis to take us back to our homes, even the junior secretaries are invited. It's one of the ways the Dents make their employees feel that they are part of the crew, one of the team. Good policy. Christmas bonus...generous leave. If you work for Dent and Dent, then Dent and Dent work for you...that is their policy.'

'I see. Any enemies?'

Masson's brow furrowed. He looked directly at Hennessey. 'Now I am worried. I have been employed by Dent and Dent for nearly twenty years and for the first time we have police officers calling on us, asking me to describe the Dents and wanting to know if they have enemies...what is happening?'

'If you'd just answer the question.'

'Oh no...oh no...' colour drained from Masson's face. 'You don't mean they are that couple...?'

'That couple?'

'The regional news, last night...the burned bodies...found at separate locations...small male, tall female...'

'We don't know yet,' Hennessey said.

'We'd appreciate it if you would keep this to yourself,' Yellich added. 'We don't want good information to be contaminated by rumour.'

'Of course...of course, I have learned to be discreet...one has to if one is a C.A.'

'Good...so...enemies?'

'None that I know of, either personally or professionally.'

'What do you know of their personal

circumstances?'

'Live quietly, as I said, two children...now grown, boy and a girl.'

'I see...Do Mr and Mrs Dent have offices in this building?'

'Yes, on the first floor, the most sought after floor.' Masson smiled. 'Above ground but not exiled to the attic. Do you want to see them?'

'In time. I think we ought to confirm that we are talking about Mr and Mrs Dent. If you could ensure no one goes in their rooms.'

'Of course. They are locked anyway.'

'Ah.' Hennessey stood. Yellich did likewise. 'So, West End House, Great Sheldwich...'

'You can't miss it...ask if you don't see it, it's *the* house of the village.'

West End House did indeed appear to both Hennessey and Yellich to be *the* house in Great Sheldwich. It was, they found, unmissable. It was not so much that it was a striking, imposing, impressive building in its own right that made it stand out, it was more its setting. Great Sheldwich appeared to be more of a hamlet than a village, with small, badly neglected cottages either side of the narrow road, some with old, decaying motorcars in the driveway. The village had but two shops, one of which was boarded up. No one, not one person was to be seen, not out of doors, not peering at the strangers from behind twitching curtains. The wind and threat of rain added to the sense of desolation.

Beyond the twin rows of small cottages stood a large house, set back from the road but clearly visible, a pocket of affluence in an area of rural poverty. Yellich drove slowly through Great Sheldwich and turned the car into the driveway of West End House. Hennessey pondered the house as they approached. Edwardian, he thought, a clear break from the cluttered roof lines so beloved of the Victorians, and a return to the graceful symmetry of the third Georgians, but not a complete return; a small window here and there and tall chimneys at either side of the building indicated its age.

Yellich halted the car beside the front door and Hennessey and he left the vehicle and walked up to the front door, which Hennessey found disappointingly small for a building the size of West End House. Hennessey pulled the bell pull and a jangling sound was heard from within the building. Hennessey and Yellich glanced at each other and then stood facing the door. It was opened, eventually, by a small, thinly built woman in a black dress. 'What?' She squinted at Yellich.

'Police,' said Hennessey, and the woman, rather than turning her head to face him, turned her body in a series of short, jerky movements. 'We'd like to speak to Mr and Mrs Dent.'

'Can't.' The woman spat the word and made to shut the door.

'Why not?' Hennessey held out his hand and prevented the door being closed.

'Not in.'

The door was then opened wider and a taller, generously proportioned woman stood in the doorway. 'Can I help, gentlemen?' Her voice was strong, confident, warm. She turned to the first woman and said, 'Thank you, Gabrielle, just carry on in the kitchen, please.'

Gabrielle scowled at Hennessey and then turned and scurried away with her arms bent at the elbow.

'Sorry,' the woman said as she smiled, 'but she comes from the village, you see.'

'Ah.' Hennessey returned the smile. 'I see.'

'And you are?'

'The police.' Hennessey showed the woman his ID. Yellich also offered his but the woman declined it with thanks saying, that if one is genuine, the other must be.

'Are Mr and Mrs Dent at home? Gabrielle said they were not at home. Is that the case?'

'Yes, it is. Would you care to come in out of the cold?' She stepped backwards and to one side, allowing Hennessey and Yellich to enter.

'Thank you.' Hennessey took his hat off as he stepped into the foyer. He found the house to be unpleasantly cold; he had expected it to be warmer.

'I am Mrs Forester. I am...well, like a butler, but we don't use the term. I manage the house for Mr and Mrs Dent.'

'I see. Really, we'd like to talk to them.'

'I'm afraid I don't know where they are. They didn't return home Thursday night, which is unusual, but nothing to panic about...but I was beginning to worry and to wonder what to do for the best. I am due home today too...I can delay my return.'

'To the village?'

'Heavens no!' Mrs Forester looked indignant at the suggestion. 'No, I live in Malton. I took this job when Mr Forester passed on. It's a live-in position but I get to return to my house each Saturday until Monday lunchtime. No, don't live in Great Sheldwich...the village is just one big family. They know who is the mother of each child that's born but the father's name on the birth certificate is a best guess. The men work on the land, the women stay at home. I never go to the village...turn right at the gate and it's a straight run to Malton. I have a car you see...I am allowed to keep it in the garage, but I wouldn't want to go into the village, it's full of Gabrielles.'

'Is there a Little Sheldwich?' Hennessey asked out of curiosity.

'There was, it was depopulated by the Black Death. A team of archaeologists from York University excavated the area, but there's nothing to see.'

'The village is that old?'

'Apparently...the present houses are mainly nineteenth century, but the site of the village is...well...ancient.'

'I see...that is interesting...just an interest of mine, you see.'

'Local history?'

'Well, yes, and other areas...but you were expecting Mr and Mrs Dent back Thursday evening?'

'Yes. They have stayed out overnight before though, but what is strange is that they always phone and let me or Mr Gregory know.'

'Mr Gregory?'

'Their son...he lives in a cottage on the estate.'

'The estate?'

'Yes, Mr and Mrs Dent own a lot of the farmland around here. They do not farm themselves, but rent the land to farmers.'

'I see...and Mr Gregory...is Gregory his Christian name?'

'Yes, Gregory Dent, but he is referred to as Mr Gregory. He might know where his parents are. I'm sure I don't...but then...oh ...they couldn't have phoned Mr Gregory, he was out last night with his young lady. Oh my, and the police asking after them. Oh...I'm going to have a turn.' She put her hand up to her mouth.

'I'm sure it's nothing to worry about, Mrs Forester.' Hennessey spoke softly. Privately he was beginning to think that there might well be much to worry about but he did not feel equipped to cope with Mrs Forester having a 'turn'. 'Would it be possible to see their bedroom?'

'Their bedroom?'

'Yes...a strange request, but I assure you there is a purpose behind it.'

'Well, they are missing...I am sure they would have phoned...it is very strange.'

'So...may we?'

'Yes...yes...' Mrs Forester turned and began to ascend the wide staircase. Hennessey and Yellich followed.

The master bedroom, as Mrs Forester referred to it as being, was of what Hennessey thought to be generous proportions, with a king-size bed opposite the door, two large wardrobes, two chests of drawers and a bathroom en suite. A dressing table stood between the bed and the first chest of drawers. Hennessey walked to the dressing table and picked up a hairbrush. 'I'd like to borrow this,' he said. 'May I?'

'Suppose...' Mrs Forester suddenly seemed to sound very weary.

'It will help us.' Hennessey took a large self-sealing cellophane sachet from his pocket and dropped the hairbrush inside. 'Tell me, Mrs Forester, what are the Dents' washing practices.'

'Washing practices?'

'Bath or shower?'

'Mrs Dent prefers to bathe...Mr Dent showers.'

'Do you mind?' Hennessey indicated the en suite bathroom. Mrs Forester meekly shook her head. Hennessey walked into the bathroom and to the shower. He pulled back the shower curtain and examined the plughole of the shower well and smiled as he did so. Taking a ballpoint from his pocket he hooked it round a small mass of hair that was trapped in the plughole. Upon examination they seemed to be short and grey. He placed them in a smaller sachet. He then returned to the bedroom. 'Do you have a recent photograph of Mr and Mrs Dent?'

'I don't think we do...the Dents are very private people. I mean, you don't move into a house in Great Sheldwich to socialize...

Dare say there is a form of community spirit in this village but it's not the sort of community I would want to be part of...oh no, dear me no...'

'Holiday snaps? Anything? It really doesn't have to be recent...anything that shows their facial appearance. Recent would be better, but not really necessary.'

'Well...in the drawing room downstairs ...perhaps...there are some photo albums.'

'Sounds ideal.'

The photograph albums, richly bound in leather, contained family snapshots showing a middle-aged couple, she significantly taller than he, occasional photographs showed a younger man and a woman with them.

'Their son and daughter,' explained Mrs Forester. 'Mr Gregory and Miss Juliette... except Miss Juliette is now Mrs Vicary.'

'They don't look like their parents.'

'They are adopted. Mr Gregory and Miss Juliette are natural brother and sister. They were adopted by the Dents when they were infants...the Dents are the only parents they have known.'

'I see...well, if I can take this photograph?' Hennessey eased a colour print from the mounting fixtures at each corner. 'It's all that we need.' He handed the photograph to Yellich who saw that it showed Mr and Mrs Dent standing together, smiling at the camera. It was a close-up photograph, showing their heads and shoulders only; a little unimaginative as a photograph but Yellich saw why Hennessey had chosen it. It would be very easy to superimpose the skull X-rays on to the faces in the photograph. They would match or they wouldn't.

'You say Mr and Mrs Dent were private people?' Hennessey addressed Mrs Forester.

'Yes, I would describe them as private... they keep themselves to themselves. All they seem to want is each other...very touching in a way ...married for all these years and still love each other.'

'Few friends, then?'

'But that doesn't mean that they are unpopular, it just means that they are...private ...like I said...a private couple.'

'Yes...enemies?'

'Oh, none that I know of, and really, I am not that close. I know them well as any housekeeper would after five years' service but not closely...not closely enough to know their enemies...if they had any, but they didn't act like a couple with enemies... always relaxed...never agitated...seemed to leave the house each morning with a certain confidence...just wanted to get to work. They seemed to care a lot for their employees.'

'Yes, we heard about the annual dinner party.'

'Oh yes, and the Christmas bonus, and a gift for each employee. It's easy to give money as a Christmas bonus but each employee got a gift as well, made them feel special...but you still haven't told me what this is all about.'

'It may all be about nothing, Mrs Forester. We'll know when we get the hair samples back to our forensic science people at Wetherby.'

'The photograph too,' Yellich added.

'Then we may or may not return. Where does Miss Juliette live...or Mrs Vicary?'

'In York.'

'And Mr Gregory.'

'On the estate, as I said. He has a cottage about a mile from here.'

'Notice anything about West End House?' Hennessey asked as he and Yellich drove away in the gathering gloom.

'No, boss.' Yellich switched the headlights on.

'It's on the east end of the village.'

'Well, that's Great Sheldwich for you,' Yellich grinned. 'Not a place I'll be visiting in my free time.'

'Nor me.'

It was Saturday, 16.17 hours.

George Hennessey's car started sluggishly. It had not after all been used all day, he being content to let Yellich drive. He drove out of the car park of Micklegate Bar police station. The traffic was heavy; it was approaching Christmas, it was Saturday. He should not be surprised, he told himself, that the traffic was so heavy, all these folk going home with Christmas gifts in the boot of their cars...and not a few, no doubt, worrying about the size of their next credit card bill. He joined the traffic stream and inched his way through the ancient city until he could escape on the A19 Thirsk Road, which by then required headlights. He drove to Easingwold and, exploiting a gap in the traffic, turned into a solid-looking detached house. From within the house a dog barked at the sound of the tyres of Hennessey's car on the gravel. Hennessey left his car and entered the house by the front door to be greeted warmly and enthusiastically by a black mongrel which he patted in return. He made himself a pot of tea and then left the house by the rear door, continuing to wear his hat and coat against the wind and the threat of rain. Oscar ran out of the open door, though a dog flap was provided for his convenience, and criss-crossed the rear lawn whilst Hennessey stood sipping a mug of tea.

'Well, this a rum one, to use an expression that amused you when you were new here, rum and no mistake. Man and woman burned...well, their corpses were incinerated, and found separately, miles apart, but they can't fail to be linked, and they are going to prove to be one Mr and Mrs Dent. We obtained hair samples from their house, from her hairbrush and the shower plughole in his case. Yellich had them sent off to Wetherby by courier; we'll get a result any time after midday Monday. Sent a photograph of the couple too, just to belt and bracer it. Somebody wanted them dead...' He sipped his tea. He loved tea when it was consumed out of doors; he found it fortifying, uplifting. 'And not just dead, but their bodies destroyed as if to prevent their being identified...so nobody was after their life insurance.' He laughed at his own joke but there was truth there. It meant that probably, just probably, immediate family could be ruled out as being not under suspicion.

But only probably.

He returned to the house and settled down in the drawing room, having shut the world out by drawing the heavy curtains, and read more of the account of the first battle of the Somme. The volume was a recent addition to his library of military history; it didn't tell him anything he didn't already know, but he did enjoy its style, a collection of written testaments from survivors, some very moving, some angry, some matter-of-fact, some with a strange, emotionless detachment about a battle which cost 60,000 British casualties in the first hour alone.

Later, he suppered on a good, wholesome stew and then, having fed Oscar, he took him for their customary walk, half an hour out to an open field, fifteen minutes for Oscar to explore off the lead, and a gentle stroll back.

Still later he walked out again...alone... into Easingwold to the Dove Inn and a pint of mild and bitter, just one before last orders were called.

Somerled and Sara Yellich sat side by side on the settee in the living room of their home in Nether Poppleton.

'Hate the weekends,' Sara said as she squeezed her husband's hand. 'He's so demanding...excited about Christmas. I can understand that, but even so, I am tempted to give in and let him soak up television. I know that's the wrong thing to do but I was close to it today...resisted, but I was close. I was so pleased when you came home. I needed that walk, that hour to myself...it freed my mind up.'

'Walking does that. I'll take him out tomorrow...I have the day off.'

'I thought you might be going in...that

case...'

'We can't do much until the identity is confirmed. We can't expect a reply from Wetherby until midday Monday. Come on, let's go up.'

'They've found them,' said the man. 'We knew they'd do that.'

'Will they identify them?' the woman asked.

'Probably...the fire went out too quickly... we didn't get the pile of ash we wanted. Should have put them in the river; let the fishes do the job for us. Should have, should have, should have...'

'Going to be a lot of that in the next few days,' she said icily. 'Going to be a lot of that in the next many years if we don't keep our heads.'

'We'll keep them,' the man said confidently. 'Don't worry, we'll keep them.'

It was Saturday, 23.10 hours.

Three

Monday, December 15,
12.30 hours – 16.15 hours
*in which the wealth of the deceased is
revealed and their family is met.*

Hennessey sat at his desk reading one report whilst Yellich sat in front of Hennessey's desk reading the other. The reports were then exchanged. Hennessey read the second report and looked up at Yellich. 'Well, that's it. As we suspected, Mr and Mrs Dent of Great Sheldwich are no longer with us.'

'Appears not. Very quick of Wetherby to come back so speedily.'

'Yes, I must write and thank them. Positive feedback, as I believe it's called, but whatever it is, it helps the world spin and we all need it. Worked under a woman once – she was a watch leader when I was in uniform – had the attitude that no comments are to be made if something goes well or someone did well but you heard about it if something went wrong; it meant all her team received nothing but adverse criticism.'

'Horrible.'

'It was. It was the most dispirited team I was in. I learned from it...learned to give positive feedback.'

'I'll remember that, boss.'

'Well...we have bad news to break. Could be interesting because, as they say, always look at the in-laws before you look at the out-laws.'

Yellich smiled. He had heard the joke before but he always appreciated the great truth it contained. 'I'll just go and grab my coat.'

Fifteen minutes later, with Yellich once again at the wheel, Hennessey and Yellich were driving along a straight but narrow road across the winter landscape of the Vale of York: blackened, freshly turned soil, denuded trees, a skein of geese under a low, grey sky. Yellich turned off the A19 and drove into Great Sheldwich. As before, not a living person was to be seen, although on that occasion – he thought probably because he was there observing – he did manage to see not one, but two net curtains twitch at their passing. Yellich drove into the driveway of West End House. The two officers left the car, walked up to the door and pulled the bell pull. The door was opened by Mrs Forester who smiled warmly at them.

'I saw you coming up the drive,' she said, 'and wanted to get to the door before Gabrielle. She means well, but social skills are not her strong point.' She then assumed a more serious looking countenance. 'I assume your return is because Mr and Mrs Dent...I mean the identification...is... What is that word? Conclusive...positive...?'

Hennessey inclined his head. 'Well...I am afraid you must continue to assume what you want to assume.'

'Oh...because I am not family?'

'Yes.'

'I see...well, that tells me everything I need to know. So you'll be looking for family?'

'Yes. You mentioned their children?'

'Mr Gregory and Miss Juliette...but they are adopted.'

'They are family in the eyes of the law. If they had been fostered they would not have been considered family,' Hennessey said, 'but having said that, are there any blood relatives?'

'Mr Dent has...or had...brothers and sisters, as did Mrs Dent.'

Hennessey and Yellich glanced at each other. Yellich said, 'They were adopted...As you say, boss, in the eyes of the law that makes them kin.'

'Yes...we could do with both.' Hennessey turned to Mrs Forester. 'Do you know where the nearest blood relatives to Mr and Mrs Dent live; nearest in terms of distance?'

'Yes, Mr Dent's brother keeps a shop in Malton High Street, a motorcycle retailer's called Dent Bikes; can't miss it. Mrs Dent has a sister in York...I have her address; I'll get it for you. Won't you please come in?' She stepped to one side and allowed Hennessey and Yellich to enter the building. It was still unpleasantly cold inside and Hennessey pondered the size of the heating bill for the house probably explained the chill.

Moments later Mrs Forester returned holding a small piece of paper which she handed to Hennessey.

'Bishopthorpe.' Hennessey read the note. 'Quite a nice area, Mrs Forester. Don't know the street, Hollyhock Avenue. Do you, Yellich?'

'Hollyhock Avenue? No...rings no bells with me, sir.'

'Very well, we'd be obliged if you would not mention our visit to anybody...anybody associated with the house or the Dents, that is.'

'Of course, I am a woman of discretion,' she replied with a smile. 'You may trust me.'

'That is appreciated.' Hennessey returned the smile. 'Well, since we are here and since the law recognizes an adopted person as next of kin...'

'You'll need to tuck your trouser bottoms into your socks.'

'Sorry?'

'Anticipating you.' Mrs Forester smiled. 'You are about to ask directions to Mr Gregory's cottage.'

'Yes.'

'Well, the car drive takes ten minutes but

the walk across the field at the back of the house takes less than five. It's very muddy this time of year, though.'

'We'll drive,' Hennessey said.

'Very well...right out of the gate, first right and first right again.'

'It'll take us more than five minutes to clean our shoes,' Yellich explained. 'It makes sense to drive there.'

'Ah...' Mrs Forester inclined her head at the logic. 'The name of the cottage is Larch Tree Cottage, white door, but it's the only building there at the end of the track.'

Both Hennessey and Yellich thought the man overacted; it was too much of a display. They were seasoned officers; they both felt they knew an act when they saw one. They had followed Mrs Forester's directions, found Larch Tree Cottage with ease, and the light from within and the smoke rising from the chimney told them that the occupier was at home. They knocked on the door and introduced themselves to the young man who answered the door. He was well built. Hennessey thought that women would be attracted to him. He broke down and wept at the news of his adoptive parents' death. He wept too much and too easily for Hennessey and Yellich to believe he was sincere in his grief.

'I knew something was wrong when they still didn't come home on Friday night. What happened?'

'Well, we were wondering if you could help us there?'

'Me?' Gregory Dent shot an alarmed look at Hennessey.

'Yes, Mr Dent, you.'

Dent sank back into his chair and gazed into the log fire. 'I...' He shook his head. 'They were my parents...I loved them very much. Why should I want to harm them?'

'How do you know they were harmed? We said nothing about them being harmed. We told you they were deceased; we said nothing about them being harmed.'

'Well...police...it must mean crime.'

'Not necessarily,' Yellich said. 'We notify of accidental death; not a pleasant duty, but we do it.'

'But that's a uniformed officer, alone. Whereas two plain clothes detectives...and senior officers...What is your rank, sir? Detective Chief Inspector, did you say?'

'Yes.'

'And you are a detective sergeant?'

'Yes.'

'Well, I don't know much about police work but I know enough to know that you two gentlemen with your rank would not call unless my parents' death was suspicious.'

Hennessey said nothing but conceded to himself that Dent had made a fair point.

'Anyway –' Dent waved a hand at the room – 'won't you take a seat? You make me feel tired looking at you stood up.'

Mumbling their thanks, Hennessey and Yellich sat in the two vacant armchairs. 'So,' Hennessey asked, 'when did you last see your parents?'

'Last see them? Friday...Thursday...Wednesday. Wednesday evening, I called on them on Wednesday. We had a matter to discuss. I left about nine o'clock. So what happened to them?'

Hennessey told him.

'That news item...' Dent pointed to a small television set which stood on a shelf beside the stone fireplace. His face paled again. 'They were burned?'

'Yes.'

'But after death…it said…after death.'

'Yes…they were not burned alive, mercifully. So, do you live here alone?'

'Yes.'

'Who owns the cottage?'

'My father owns it, or at least he did.'

'And with your mother also deceased, who will inherit your father's estate?'

'Well, the will has to be read but…' Hennessey thought Dent looked smug. 'I dare say me and my sister will get the lion's share …dare say that's some compensation for losing your parents.'

'I understand that you and your sister were adopted?'

'Yes. We were old enough to understand right from the outset. My parents couldn't have children, so they adopted a pair. I was five, my sister seven when we came to live at West End House. Our real name is Locke… with an *e*. Our parents…our natural parents, were killed in a car crash. The story was that my father was a keen rugby player, had a game, got drunk after the game, phoned my mother up to collect him, she took a taxi there, poured him into the back seat with the help of his mates, then less than a mile later they were dead. Killed outright in a collision with a lorry driven by a Frenchman. It was on the wrong side of the road. The frog didn't turn up for the trial and all the judge could do was to issue a warrant for his arrest if he set foot in the UK again; the European arrest warrant didn't exist back then. So, we were shipped off to a children's home. That was alright...wasn't anything special. I have no complaints about it. Then we were put up for adoption, the Dents visited us...The children's home was in Hull, you see. They signed the papers and we became Gregory and Juliette Dent. We had more trouble adapting to life in West End House than life in the children's home. We were what you'd call working class...East Hull...know it?'

'Not really...been there a couple of times,' Hennessey said.

'Same,' Yellich added.

'Well, we took to the children's home because we spoke their language, in their accent, but the Dents were upper middle class...we had some adjusting to do, and then they packed us off to boarding school.

Just minor public schools, mine was in Cumbria, near Carlisle. Juliette went to one in Norfolk. Lucky her, quite near Norwich. Do you know Norwich?'

'Can't say I do.' Hennessey was content to let Dent talk. He noticed the apparent grief had rapidly evaporated.

'Me neither.'

'Lovely city.' Dent smiled as if recollecting a pleasant memory. 'But not Carlisle...drab place...the only good thing about Carlisle was the railway station, not because that's the way out, but because it's always busy. We used to be able to go out of school on Saturday afternoons and I would often go the railway station just to watch the trains. Such a busy station; trains coming and going all the time...from north and south...east and west...passenger as well as goods traffic. That was my escape from school, but Juliette did better. She made friends at school, unlike me, and had Norwich to visit on Saturdays and public holidays.'

'Are you employed, Mr Dent?'

'You mean, what am I doing sitting at home in the middle of the afternoon on a weekday?'

'No...no...I meant are you employed?' Hennessey spoke solemnly. 'Many shift workers sit at home on a weekday afternoon.'

'OK, point to you. Yes, I am employed. I manage the campsite.'

'Campsite? Tents?'

'No...I should call it the caravan site. We have a site of static caravans, fifty static caravans out by Filey. People from Leeds and Sheffield rent them for a fortnight at a time with their children. Confess I wouldn't keep a dog in one but they're happy enough. The work is seasonal, keeps me busy in summer, then the site is shut down, some routine maintenance to enable the vans to weather the winter. That wind off the North Sea, I swear you'd think the vans were being attacked with crowbars...One little crack and the wind gets in and widens it, so we repaint the vans as soon as the season is over, put bitumen on the roofs, seal them for the winter. When that's done, there is nothing else to do until the spring when the vans are valeted before the season starts. They're fenced in...and we have an old man keeping his eye on them in case the vandals get in, but they never do. The locals know that there's nothing in the vans...and who's going to go on the cliff top on a wild night in February just to break a few windows for a laugh? So they're safe...like my friend's sheep.'

'Sheep?' Hennessey glanced at the fire as a log crackled.

'School friend...made a fortune in the City, just bought and sold at the right times, then went green and bought an island in the Orkneys with just one house on it...quite a large house...put some sheep on the island which was criss-crossed with drystone walls and gateways in the walls allowing the sheep to roam all over the island. In the winter he and his girlfriend head south to France, the Mediterranean coast of same...leaving the sheep to fend for themselves.'

'They can do that?'

'Apparently...you see, there's very little snow in the Orkneys because of the sea's influence, so the sheep can always reach the grass, keep themselves well fed. There are no predators on the island, and the criss-crossing nature of the walls means that the sheep can always find a lee of a wall to shelter behind, no matter which way the wind blows. Rupert, my friend, and his girl-friend return in the spring for lambing. They're very green wellie, wax jacket types when in the Orkneys. So my vans are like his sheep. In the winter they fend for them-selves.'

'And you put your feet up in front of a log fire?'

'Hard life, isn't it?' Gregory Dent smiled a very self-satisfied smile, Hennessey thought, very self-satisfied, too self-satisfied. A 'cat that got the cream' sort of satisfaction, a 'can't-touch-me' expression. Hennessey had seen that expression many times, and many times he had disabused the wearer of the idea.

'But I do have other responsibilities. I am supposed to be the family member in charge of the house,' he pointed to West End House. 'Both my parents working, you see...but Mrs Forester is so...efficient...she does my job for me.'

'So you sit at home?'

'Most days in the winter. In the summer I have to be at the van site...my own little box to live in and those people who knock on your door at all hours, speaking in dialect, complaining about this and that. I am twenty-seven years old, I have got better things to do with my summers than spend them in Filey and with no end in sight...and there's Rupert Fullerton with his island in the Orkneys bought and paid for and his house in the south of France, also bought and paid for...same age as me...set for life.' His chin set firm, 'the cat that got the cream' look evaporated and was replaced by an expression that said 'injustice' and 'gross unfairness'.

'Time to do something about it,' Hennessey suggested.

'Well, things are now quite different... overnight they are different. I am sorry for the parents, they pulled us out of that children's home...Sycamore Lodge it was called.'

'Sycamore Lodge,' Hennessey repeated.

'East Hull...forget the name of the road. We were there for nearly a year...Hughes Street Primary School.'

'Hughes Street?'

'Yes...I wasn't unhappy there, better than at Brookfield.'

'Brookfield?'

'My boarding school, up by Carlisle from where I used to catch the bus into Carlisle, get off by the citadel, buy a platform ticket and spend the afternoon on the platforms of the railway station...Trains from north and south and east and west, remember. Wasn't a trainspotter though. Could never see the point in writing train numbers into a little book.'

'So...your father had a business interest outside the accountancy practice?'

'Yes...not just the van site. He owned a garage, a petrol filling station, not a repair garage. He doesn't...didn't know enough about cars to run a repair garage; and he has a car park; that is money for nothing; concrete a bit of land and charge people to park their cars on it. I mean, what could be an easier way of making money? He owns a few houses he rents to students...another money-spinner; students pay for the house, you own it. Then he has quite a portfolio of stocks and shares...So he's worth a little money.'

'Any enemies?'

'What businessman doesn't have enemies? Seems the more successful you are, the more enemies you make. Seems like that anyway.'

'Anyone in particular?'

'I wasn't close enough to the heart of things to know.'

'I see...but you'll benefit from his death?'

'Oh...I hope so...' Again he smiled. Hennessey saw that 'the cat that got the cream' look had reappeared. 'I do hope so.'

'So where were you on Thursday evening?'

'With my girlfriend.'

'Where were you?'

'At her house. Alone.'

'Just the two of you?'

'Just the two of us.'

'We'll have to confirm that with her. And we'll also have to speak with your sister. If you could give us their addresses?'

'Gladly.' Gregory Dent stood and once again revealed himself to be a lithe and a muscular young man.

'Gregory phoned. He said you'd call.' The woman seemed pale, drawn. Hennessey thought she was in shock. 'Mummy and Daddy...you'd better come in.'

Hennessey and Yellich stepped over the

threshold into what seemed to Hennessey to be a modest family home. The woman invited them into the living room and began to pick up cushions and put them down again, run her fingers through her hair and turn away from the officers and turn towards them again.

'We could call later,' Hennessey offered.

'No...no, please...I want to know what happened...Mummy and Daddy...please take a seat.'

Hennessey and Yellich sat in an armchair each, the woman sat on the settee chewing her nails. She wore faded denim jeans, sports shoes, a man's rugby shirt patterned in brown and yellow horizontal stripes. Her hair was combed back and fashioned into a small ponytail. Hennessey read the room. It was a little untidy, more 'lived in' he thought than abandoned, it was clean, prints of the French Impressionists hung on the wall. The room smelled of air freshener and furniture polish, but faintly so.

'You are Mr and Mrs Dent's adopted daughter?'

'Yes, Mrs Vicary, Juliette Vicary. My husband teaches at Trinity College, not as grand as it sounds...it isn't Trinity College, Cambridge, nor even Trinity College, Dublin, but Trinity and St Joseph's College of Education. It produces primary school teachers. My husband teaches a course in history. As well as developmental psychology and such, the students have to major in one academic subject...my husband teaches those who choose history.'

'I see.'

'He's not at home...he'll be back at about five if you need to talk to him.'

'Not really,' Hennessey spoke softly. 'I don't think there's any need to speak to your husband at all. We really want to know more about Mr and Mrs Dent.'

'Yes...but who would want to harm them?'

'Is the question we would like answering too...who would? Do you know?'

Juliette Vicary shook her head. 'No...no...I know of no enemies of theirs but Daddy had a finger in a lot of pies. He was more than just an accountant...he was a businessman.'

'So we found out...quite an empire.'

'Oh...hardly anything.' She forced a smile. 'I mean in the great scheme of things, hardly a multinational corporation. He was a small fish, very local, no business interests outside York. I don't think he planned to... Mind, he was looking forward to his retirement, so his planning days were over.'

'What was he going to do with his business ...his businesses?'

'I really don't know.'

'You and Gregory wouldn't take anything over?'

'Oh, no.' She smiled and then glanced out of the window. 'No, I am the wife of a history teacher and we both want to start a family. I have no time to run a business, I am just not that sort to be a businesswoman, swanning around in a Jaguar. I doubt my learned husband would approve anyway. He thinks that teaching is a noble profession; he likes working for a salary. He has often said he wouldn't work in the private sector, he wouldn't want to work for the profit motive.'

'I see.' Hennessey relaxed in the armchair. He was struck by how different Juliette Vicary seemed to be from her brother. He detected the family resemblance, both tall, he well built, she not big boned, but not finely made either, and there, he thought, the resemblance ended. His first impression of this woman was that she was warm and genuine, while the impression he had of her brother was that he was neither. 'And your brother, would he have become responsible for your father's local empire upon Mr Dent's retirement?'

Juliette Vicary's head sank forward. She looked uncomfortable. 'No...you may as well know that ours wasn't a particularly happy home. I seemed to get on alright with Mummy and Daddy...I did well at school...I didn't want to go to university, I worked on a kibbutz for a while to get some life experience...sort of find myself, met Leonard and my parents approved the match. It's been a good ten years for Leonard and me...Children are a bit delayed, we've been trying... there's still time...but Gregory and Daddy... I think he was a disappointment to them... not Daddy's fault, nor Mummy's. You adopt a child...you adopt someone else's creation ...but Gregory is feckless. That's it, he's my brother – full brother – and he is feckless.'

'He manages a campsite of static caravans.'

'Does he?' Juliette Vicary raised her eyebrows. 'You know him.'

'We do?'

'Yes...well, the police at Filey do. He stole money from the safe in the manager's office...quite a lot of money...two thousand pounds.'

'And he's still allowed to keep his job?'

'He has to be given a job...a nominal job, so Daddy thinks. If he doesn't, he'll only get into more trouble with you gentlemen. It keeps him out of trouble. Letting him think he's got a job and giving him a salary and a place to live...rent free as well, he pays nothing for his cottage, he's kept. If it wasn't for a man at the site, a man called Mayhew, Clarence Mayhew, the caravan rental business would have gone under years ago. He is the under manager of the site but to all intents and purposes he is *the* manager. I'm sorry, I am in a bit of a state...'

'Yes, I can appreciate how difficult this is for you.'

'Well, answering the questions isn't difficult...absorbing what has happened is. It doesn't seem real...it's like a dream. I am sure you see this all the time.'

'A few times.' Hennessey smiled. 'Not all

the time, thank goodness...that would be too much to cope with.'

'I can imagine...but you see life.'

'Yes.'

'That's what an Israeli soldier once said to me on the kibbutz...soldiers don't get paid much but we see life.'

'Dare say we can say the same. So who would know the extent of your father's business dealings?'

'Only Daddy. His papers will be in the premises of the accountancy firm, but you'll need to be a Philadelphia lawyer to get to grips with them.'

'Dare say we could cope. Do we have your permission to look at them?'

'Do you need my permission?' She held her palm against her chest.

'Yes...either yours or Gregory's.'

'You are the surviving heirs,' Yellich explained.

'Oh, I suppose I am...I haven't thought that far ahead.' She glanced at the window, distracted by the sound of a car drawing to a halt outside her house. 'It's my husband; I phoned him at work...I told him about Mummy and Daddy...I told him you would be calling...He's obviously been able to get away. Excuse me.' Juliette Vicary stood and walked hurriedly out of the door.

Hennessey and Yellich heard the front door open and Juliette Vicary say, 'Oh, Leonard, the police are here,' and a male voice then issued words of comfort. The door shut with a click and a man walked down the entrance hall and stood in the living room.

'Mr Vicary?' Hennessey stood. Yellich did likewise.

'Yes.' He extended his hand. 'Please be seated, gentlemen,' he said as he shook Hennessey's hand with a firm but not a crushing grip. He sat on the settee; Juliette sat beside him, nestling into him. 'This is a tragedy,' he said, 'a real tragedy.'

'Yes.' Hennessey nodded. 'Two lives. Any life taken before its due time is a tragedy, even elderly people, and a married couple still with much to live for...yes, a tragedy.'

'Yes...what happened?'

'Well.' Hennessey sank back on to the settee, 'details, as they say, are sketchy. Both were killed before they were incinerated.'

'Thank goodness.' Leonard slid his hand into his wife's. 'Sorry, I didn't mean it to sound like that...I am just grateful that they were not burned alive; that would be too terrible to contemplate.'

'It's alright.' Hennessey held up his palm. 'I know what you meant. We had the same fear and the same sense of relief, but one, Mr Dent, appeared to have been killed by a massive blunt trauma to the head. Mrs Dent appeared to have been strangled.'

'Oh...' Juliette's hand went up to her mouth. 'Mummy.' Leonard Vicary slid his arm round her shoulders and pulled her closer to him.

'Little else is known, so we're at the stage of tracing their last movements and inquiring into any person who might have had a motive to harm them.'

'Harm! I think they did a bit more than harm.' Leonard Vicary seemed to Hennessey to cut a striking figure; he was a man who appeared to be in his late thirties, he had a full head of white hair which was swept back and balanced with a striking white beard and moustache, and between them sat a strongly pointed nose. He spoke with an accent foreign to Yorkshire. Midlands, thought Hennessey, north of London but south of Birmingham, that sort of area. 'But anything we can do to help,' Leonard continued.

'So, just to eliminate you, where were you last Thursday evening?'

'Home...here.' Leonard Vicary spoke with finality.

'Just the two of you?'

'Yes...it's a pattern that has established itself during term time, especially towards the end of term as now. It's the job...I love teaching but it takes from you. At the end of the week, all I want to do is collapse in front of the television. Just me and Juliette and a bottle of chilled Frascati, before and during a meal and then a very early night...I mean about nine p.m., probably nine thirty or ten ...We also stay in on Fridays and Saturdays. The town is full of youth then but Sunday evenings, when said youth is paying for the previous evening, and the pubs are quiet, then we stroll out to the Lockkeepers' Arms ...know it?'

'No.'

'Near here...real ale...no music...no smoking allowed anywhere. A real gem of a pub ...but Thursday we were at home...home alone...just we two...just as we like it.'

'Just soaking up television?'

'Well, soaking up the screen...Don't watch a lot of television...Video we rented from the video shop or a DVD from the DVD shop.'

'What did you watch?'

'*My Father's Den*...New Zealand film... quite good.'

'I'll keep an eye out for it. So...you knew little of Mr and Mrs Dent's business dealings?'

'Little, close to nothing,' Leonard Vicary answered, 'especially me, I had...still have, no interest in the Dent Corporation.'

'It's hardly a corporation,' Juliette Vicary said as she glanced at her husband. 'A few small businesses in and around York...and it's not fair...they're dead, murdered...it's not fair to dismiss them like that anymore.'

'Sorry, sorry...' He squeezed her shoulders gently. 'Sorry.'

'You didn't approve of your parents-in-law?'

'I liked them as a couple – provided me with a beautiful wife – but I am not interested in business. I am a man of modest beginnings. I am proud of my degree, our little house, all bought and nearly paid for by education, education and education... That's my world...not the world of finance and property and profit...So I especially, and we as a couple, know nothing of Mr and Mrs Dent's business dealings.'

'And it's only Daddy.'

'Sorry?'

'Only Daddy,' Juliette Vicary explained. 'It was only Daddy who had business interests; Mummy was a partner in the accountancy practice but not in anything else.'

'Ah...I see...so the person to ask is at the practice...back on Precenters Court?'

'Yes.'

'So when did you last see your parents?'

The Vicarys glanced at each other. 'Last weekend,' Juliette answered. 'We drove out for Sunday lunch...that's also a pattern...not every Sunday.'

'About once a month,' Leonard Vicary explained. 'About...not a regular as clockwork thing.'

'Did you and Mr and Mrs Dent have a good relationship, as son-in-law and parents-in-law?'

Vicary glanced at his wife, who held eye contact with him. She nodded slightly. Vicary then turned to Hennessey and said, 'Yes...yes, I did. He is a wealthy man... Sorry, was a wealthy man, and like all wealthy men, he naturally suspected my motives when he was told Juliette and I had got engaged.'

'He was worried that you might be after his money?'

'Yes, that thought must have crossed his mind and he tested me...he provided a modest dowry for Juliette and then left a substantial sum of money in a trust fund to be shared equally by his grandchildren upon their reaching the age of twenty-seven.'

'Twenty-seven?'

'Too young and they'll squander it...that was his thinking. I think he was right. If I was given a million...'

'A million!'

'I said it was a substantial sum of money.' Vicary smiled. 'If we have four children, they'll inherit a million each...if we have three...or two...or one...any equal shares of four million pounds.'

'And if we don't have children, we'll

adopt,' Juliette Vicary added helpfully. 'That's a bit of a family tradition.'

'I see.' Hennessey smiled. 'I see.'

'And when he also found out that I was interested only in pursuing a career in teaching and not wanting to edge my way into his business empire, then I met with his approval and married his beautiful daughter.' Leonard and Juliette Vicary beamed at each other. 'So our relationship was warm... we enjoyed Sunday lunch at West End House.'

'So you won't benefit from his death or that of Mrs Dent either?'

'That remains to be seen...he might have left us a few drops of drinking water, but we are advised the flood has gone to a trust fund to give to human beings who have yet to be born.'

'The accountancy practice has no selling value,' Juliette Vicary explained. 'It's like a law firm; the money comes in from clients, keeps the owners and employees in work, but upon the owner's death or retirement, the firm will be wound up, the employees will find other positions, the clients other accountants. Only the premises will have some value but the concept of the business ...none at all.' She paused. 'Oh...this is really ...all too much to take on board, I still can't believe it...This morning Mummy and Daddy were alive...so I thought...now I am...now they are deceased and those news reports about the man and woman being burned...well, their bodies were burnt. I never, never in my wildest dreams thought... life has got very real...it feels very solid, colours are louder. I looked at the front lawn before you gentlemen arrived and I found beauty in a blade of grass. I read that once,that a dying man can find beauty in a blade of grass. Well, I can tell you that suddenly bereaved people can find the same beauty in the same place...and yet you know, there is a dream-like quality to it all. I really need to lie down...Would you mind?'

'No.' Hennessey stood, Yellich also. 'This has been very useful...it has helped us.'

'Helped?' Leonard Vicary also stood. 'I can't see what we have done to help.'

'Background information...helped us to get the measure of the Dent household out there at Great Sheldwich...all grist to the mill.'

'Well, you know where we are if you think we can help you further.'

'Indeed.'

'I'll see you out.'

Bernard Masson furrowed his brow. 'Do you have that authorization in writing?'

'No,' Hennessey replied. 'Sorry, no...it's verbal but given before my sergeant here.' He indicated to Yellich who sat beside him in front of Masson's desk.

'If you don't mind...' Masson reached forward and picked up the phone on his desk, 'I'll confirm it. Ah, Penny, can you please phone Mr and Mrs Dent's daughter...the number is in our directory under V. Yes, Vicary.. .thanks, I'll hold. Sorry, but I must be certain you have the permission.'

'Of course.' Hennessey nodded. 'I would do the same.'

'Good of you. Oh...Juliette, sorry to disturb you, it's Bernard. May I say how sorry I am...we all are really...well, the police are here...' Moments later he replaced the phone and said, 'Well, as you say, on the authorization of their daughter and eldest child, you may have full access to all the

106

papers in respect of the late Anthony Dent's business dealings. The only spare accommodation is Mr Dent's office...or Mrs Dent's... bit like stepping into dead men's shoes.'

'Are you familiar with Mr Dent's business dealings?'

'His little empire?' Masson pursed his lips. 'I think I am...unless anything major has been withheld from me...I think I am.'

'We'll look at the documents, of course, but could you give us some idea of what we will find?'

'Lots of small businesses with low overheads and little time needed to devote to the management of same. Anthony's time was consumed almost wholly by the practice.' Masson tapped his desktop. 'This was his passion. He built it from scratch. He was a recently qualified accountant and was working for Wheeler, Perkins and Walsh – they have premises in St Leonard's Place, big firm, good firm but got a bit sloppy with one of their clients, a landowner, a gentleman farmer in the old tradition. Anthony phoned this gentleman one day, one weekend from his home and asked, "How would you like to receive a quarter of a million pounds?"

This was some thirty years ago remember, probably two or three million in today's terms. The client replied, "What do I have to do?" "Nothing," says Anthony, "just give me your account." Turns out that the gentleman had been paying far too much tax. Wheeler, Perkins and Walsh just were not doing their job...they'd put a sloppy junior in charge of the account and for years he'd been paying far too much to the Exchequer. So Anthony set up alone, the client moved his account to Dent and Dent. Muriel and he were not yet married, though they were an item, and Anthony came up with the goods and this gentleman received a massive rebate. Christmas came early for him that year. Word spread and Anthony won some very wealthy clients among the land-owning set in West and North Yorkshire. The cloth-capped pigeon-fancier typical Yorkshireman who goes to bed sucking on a rod of mild steel, well, that belongs to South Yorkshire...possibly Leeds and Bradford as well, but in the Vale and the Dales there is some very serious old money...And Dent and Dent is *the* accountants to have. We are proud of our reputation...Our clients stay with us.'

'So how much are...were the Dents worth?'

'Pencil figure?'

'Alright.'

'All in...probably about ten.'

'Ten?'

'Million.'

Hennessey gasped. 'I knew he was well off, but not that well off.'

'Well, it's what he's worth in terms of his property portfolio. There is West End House ...and that is a lot of property. It's not just the house, you see, it's the farmland that surrounds the house, then there is the caravan site...'

'Gregory's little area of responsibility.'

'Yes. Anthony did not just own all the caravans on the site, he also owned the site itself; that's quite a few acres of cliff top. If planning permission could be obtained to build on that, a hotel perhaps, then it would be worth a great deal of money. Then there is this building –' Masson waved a hand with an upturned palm – 'excellent condition, Regency, smack in the centre of York overlooking the Minster grounds. Already you are into six figures. Then there are the car parks...small by comparison, but city centre sites, again with planning permission ...who knows what they could be worth?' Masson paused. 'Then there's land...'

'More land?'

'Oh yes, it's all land. Low maintenance business; farms that are let to tenant farmers for a modest rent, but Anthony owned the land, acres of private woodland, stretches of river banks on which he sells annual angling permits to use. The car parks are private, not staffed, they have a barrier across the entrance and each person that rents a space has a key. So no need to have somebody there collecting the parking fees. The land he owns doesn't generate a great deal of income, but it's the fact that he owns it that makes him wealthy.'

'I see...so who would benefit from his death?'

Masson opened his hands and shrugged. 'I suppose that depends on his will. If he didn't leave it all to a cat's home and made a logical will, then in the event of the common calamity I would assume that his adoptive son and daughter would become handsomely well off.'

'Very handsomely, I'd say,' commented Yellich.

'What do you know of his children?' asked Hennessey.

'Little. Met both but know little.'

'Did Mr Dent ever speak of his children?'

'Often, as any parent would...not worried about Juliette, she made a good marriage to a man who is not interested in the business, but Gregory...Anthony was worried about him...called him feckless. He really didn't see Gregory doing anything for the business. Come to think of it, ten might be an underestimate...might be nearer fifteen... possibly above fifteen. Well, I'll get the papers.' Masson stood. 'Tell you who to talk to...'

'Oh?'

'Anthony's brother...out in Malton, owns a motorcycle retail outlet.'

'Yes, we have heard of him.'

'They were close...he and Anthony. If Anthony did say anything of relevance, it would have been to his brother.'

'Thursday night? Last week?' The woman

extended a slender finger upwards and then to her right as if indicating 'last week' was outside her home, somewhere in the narrow street. She was slender, like her finger, a mop of black hair over a balanced face. She kept the central heating turned up so that on a day like that day, she was comfortable in a red T-shirt and cut down jeans. One leg she folded underneath her as she sat, the other extended until her bare foot rested on the varnished floorboards. Her home was a modest terraced house within the walls of the city, where it is said that there is a church for every Sunday in the year and a pub for every other day.

Hennessey and Yellich sat side by side on the sofa, being the only other seating available in the cramped room.

'Yes. I presume Mr Dent phoned you to tell you we'd be calling?'

'He might have done but I have only just returned from work. So, Thursday last week?'

'Yes.'

'You know, I find it difficult to recall, it's the sign of a busy life...I am a legal secretary. Let's see, Monday today, yesterday was a lazy day. I don't work on a Sunday, not out of any religious conviction, I just don't lift a finger...not even any washing up. The washing up from yesterday's meals still waits for me in the kitchen, a great pile of it. Saturday...Saturday I shopped, began to eat away at my Christmas shopping list.' She glanced at her ceiling of mauve painted plaster. 'I dread my credit card bill; it's going to be a belt-tightening winter for this little spendthrift. I come from a large family with many relatives to buy for. So, that was Saturday...spent Saturday evening wrapping them up, then had an early night. Friday...at work all day...I work at Banks and Webb.'

'I don't know that firm.'

'They don't do criminal work, there's no money in it, so you probably wouldn't have heard of them. Just civil law work.'

'I see.'

'So Friday night I stayed in...Thursday... yes, Gregory was here, we both had a quiet night in. He stayed the night and left when I went to work. He returned to the mausoleum.'

'The mausoleum?'

'That's what Gregory calls West End

House.'

'So...tell us, Miss Thurnham...'

'Mrs. Sorry, I am Mrs Thurnham. I am separated...divorce pending. When I am divorced, I will return to my maiden name of Moss. Susan Moss. Can't wait to return, my maiden name makes me feel clean. My marriage was short and unpleasant; the name of Thurnham makes me feel contaminated.' She shrugged. 'Anyway, tell you what?'

'Are you a long time associate of Mr Dent's?'

'We've known each other for about six months, known each other in the biblical sense for about four...being of course the last four.'

'I see.'

'I was reluctant to get involved with anyone so soon after separating from Baron William the brute, of York, but Gregory has a charm about him, and I have my needs. I want many pleasant memories to comfort me when I am in my rocking chair.'

'Aye,' Hennessey sighed, 'none of us get younger, except Merlin the Magician, and growing old is no fun but it's distinctly preferable than the alternative. So you haven't seen Gregory Dent since the news of his parents' murder?'

'No...I didn't know whether to call or not. I am not very skilled on such occasions... Sometimes...well, my parents are very cautious people and they told me over and over again: "if you don't know what to do, do nothing" or as they said, "if in doubt do nowt". So I did nowt. Gregory knows where I am if he needs me.'

'Alright...do you know much about his relationship with his parents?'

Susan Thurnham shrugged. 'Not good... edgy...I think there were arguments. Gregory complained that they were holding him back. He wanted more of his father's business empire; he felt it was rightfully his.'

'He did?'

'Yes...all he got was a silly management position at the caravan site on the cliff top. He wanted more than that; he's very ambitious, impatient to get on, but his parents are...or were...blocking him, so he said.'

'Interesting.'

'What happens now, I don't know. It will be dependent upon what his parents left him in their will, I suppose.'

'Indeed. Mrs Thurnham, I have to tell you this, that anybody who provides a false alibi is liable to prosecution as an accessory.'

She raised her eyebrows and smiled. 'Is that a fact?'

'Yes.' Hennessey stood. Yellich did likewise. 'Yes, it's a fact.'

Four

Tuesday, December 16,
09.00 – 16.30 hours
*in which the good Chief Inspector has
old wounds unintentionally opened and
later meets a sputnik, and Yellich views an
illuminating photograph.*

'Dad advised them against it.' Robin Dent sat at his desk, reclining in his chair. Hennessey cast an eye round the office. He saw it to be neat, efficient-looking, a little characterless, he thought. Behind Dent was a calendar of photographs of motorbikes. December's photograph was of a powerful looking yellow machine with a leggy girl in a Father Christmas jacket and hat sitting astride it.

Hennessey felt uncomfortable in the shop.

Personal, deeply felt and unpleasant memories resonated. 'Really?'

'Really.' Robin Dent was, Hennessey noted, like his deceased brother, short in stature. 'Yes, really,' he smiled. There was, thought Hennessey, a warmth about the man. 'Mind you, Dad advised me against buying my first bike and look where it got me.' He looked around him. 'I haven't got the money that Anthony had with his empire but I have done well...pulled myself up. We are both of humble origins; never had a lot when we were growing up. It makes you lust for wealth, not easy money, but money. There is moral money and immoral money. Dad was a lay preacher, a Methodist, was always one for the right and the wrong of it. Talked about giving and the importance to give of yourself. I could quite understand it when he didn't want me to get a motorbike, few parents like their children having bikes but really they are as safe as their rider.'

And that, thought Hennessey with anger, is not true. It isn't true at all. He managed to remain silent. He breathed in through his nose and smelled a cocktail of air freshener and furniture polish with a whiff of new leather, new metal and new rubber.

'So...' Dent continued, 'it was something of a surprise when he advised Anthony and Muriel against adopting. He said, you just do not know what you are bringing into the family, you do not know what damaged goods you are taking on board. You can't make a silk purse out of a sow's ear, that was his most often used phrase, which we thought strange. He was all for giving of yourself, helping others. We thought adopting a couple of orphaned children would have a place within his philosophy but how wrong we were. His notion of giving did not extend to compromising his own. He had a shrewdness about him which we only found out when Anthony and Muriel announced their intention to adopt.'

'Interesting.'

'Yes...it was...you're twenty plus and you find out something about your parents for the first time...it's a revelation.'

'So there was not a great age gap between your brother and sister-in-law and their adoptive children?'

'No...the age gap was enough to be parent

and child but it wasn't a massive gap...but enough.'

'They gave up easily, or was there a clear medical reason for not having children?'

'Gave up?'

'Trying for a family.'

'Ah...no...they tried...had tests and found out that Anthony was sterile, he'd never have children. That was a massive blow to Muriel...worse than if she was unable to have children, so she said, because she was able to reproduce but would never have children on her own...but she loved Anthony. It was a sacrifice she was prepared to make. Good for her, I say.'

'Yes, a noble gesture.'

'Not like our parents...there was quite a gap between us and them, particularly Dad. He was an elderly father but a strong man, just went on and on. He was killed...'

'I'm sorry.'

'So were we...he was knocked down by a motorcyclist. Ironically the motorcyclist bought his machine from this outlet. I sold a young man a machine that he rode into my father...It has given me something to think about.'

'I'll say.'

'But most of the bikes you see round here are purchased from me and it probably was Dad's fault. He stepped into the path of the biker – there were witnesses – and the biker wasn't doing anything wrong. The police didn't prosecute him; says a lot.'

'Yes.'

'He was tipped to make the century eventually, get a telegram from Buckingham Palace...but he had had a long life and he had lived it well, so his funeral was still a celebration of a life. He was eighty-four, so he might have been short-changed a little... but only a little.'

'Yes.' Hennessey nodded. 'Short-changed but only a little.' Again, difficult memories echoed and chimed, again anger at the unfairness of it all gripped at his chest.

'Well, he was very upset when he heard about Gregory and Juliette having been found in a children's home in East Hull. He said the Americans have a saying, "You can take the kid out of the ghetto, but you can't take the ghetto out of the kid".'

'Yes, thank you...I was aware of that.'

'Well, he seemed to have been proved

correct. Anthony once said that he wondered what sort of monster we had brought into this family.'

'Meaning?' Hennessey sat forward.

'Meaning Gregory. He and Muriel never seemed to be worried about Juliette...but Gregory was always very difficult. There was always something amoral about him. If he wasn't given anything he'd take it but he wouldn't see it as stealing...tried to find a rationalization. He just wouldn't see it as theft, or lack of responsibility, or whatever. He'd been given a job to do, and he wouldn't do it because nobody else had been given a similar job...this was when he was a boy. Juliette would be given a reward for something; he'd take the same thing as his reward...played according to his own rules, which he made up to suit himself as he went along.'

'I have met the type.'

'Yes...in your line of work I imagine you have. But Anthony was fearful. He once said he thought that Dad had been right, he said he feared great trouble from Gregory...That was when he was still quite young, and the problem with adopting is that you can't unadopt easily. ..and you can't split up siblings. They couldn't keep Juliette and send Gregory back, so they kept him, sent him to a Roman Catholic boarding school in the hope that a good infusion of popery would instil some sense of right and wrong in him.'

'Do you know how he got on at school?'

Robin Dent shook his head. 'I don't... Anthony never spoke about it, but Gregory left as soon as he could with few, if any, qualifications...he never mentioned any school friends to me. Seemed to come home expecting Anthony and Muriel to provide for him. Never took a job...Technically – legally – they could have shown him the door on his sixteenth birthday but that was either not in their nature...or...and I hesitate to say this...or they were by then already frightened of him.'

'Had they reason to fear him?'

'Well, nothing was said but I did suspect he had been violent, more likely towards Anthony, but probably Muriel as well, and Anthony told me of the cats that went missing, often coincidental with the sound of a shotgun being discharged.'

'They had a firearm?'

123

'A 410...licensed...to keep the vermin down on the farm.'

'Alright.'

'But over a period of twelve months, the four cats they had disappeared. At the time each one disappeared, Gregory was seen with the 410 as if busying himself shooting rats...and rabbits...and magpies...maybe a fox; that was the sort of job Gregory would do...use the 410, but anything constructive, long term, anything requiring a level of responsibility, no way, not Gregory.'

'How did the animals in the house react to him?'

'They kept out of his way. The old Labrador they had growled at him the moment he entered the house, and the little boy that he was then, he smiled at the dog growling at him, a really sinister smile. The dog died soon afterwards.'

'Interesting.'

'Isn't it? I thought you people always visited in pairs?'

'Not always, only when visiting suspects.' Hennessey stood. 'And you are not a suspect...just a provider of background information.'

'That's a relief.' Robin Dent also stood and he and Hennessey shook hands. 'Can't interest you in a motorbike? You don't see yourself as a "grey biker"? I am selling a lot of machines to retired couples and single men.'

Hennessey withdrew his hand. 'Definitely not.'

Yellich also collected background information. Mabel Johnson sat pale and drawn looking in her neatly kept house in Fulford. 'There was just the two of us, Muriel and Mabel Cross, the cross sisters...used to be a joke, you know like the one "I sometimes wake up bad tempered but mostly I let him sleep". A bit like that. We were the "cross sisters".'

Yellich smiled.

'My Nigel was a good man but he never amounted to much in life. This was what he achieved, this little house, before it pleased the Lord to take him from me. We sort of stayed still in life. Muriel and I grew up in a house like this, modest you might say. Nigel too grew up like this, lived like this...and... well, it isn't my turn yet, so I still live like this but Muriel did very well in her marriage...on every level. She and Anthony loved each other, they really were inseparable and what Anthony achieved...and to die like that. The paper said they were dead before they were burnt, is that correct?'

'Yes.' Yellich glanced around him. The house he saw was neatly but very prosaically decorated. He thought that there was little evidence of much, if any, imagination in the lifestyle of Mrs Johnson and her late husband, Nigel.

'Yes, that was the case.'

'Can you tell that? How?' Mabel Johnson was a frail looking lady, who, Yellich thought, was dressed older than her years. It was, he thought, as if old age had some appeal for her, some attraction and, unusually, she was anxious to reach it. But that, he thought, was better than middle-aged women who wore the short skirts of a teenager.

'Yes...if there are soot deposits in the trachea...'

'Trachea?'

'The throat. If there are soot deposits there it means the person breathed in smoke, which means they were alive when engulfed in flames...No smoke in the trachea means that the person was not breathing when they were...'

'Engulfed in flames.' Mabel Johnson finished the sentence for Yellich. 'I see...and my sister and her husband had no smoke in their...trachea?'

'None.'

'You are not just saying that to comfort me?'

'No...' Yellich smiled again as he sat in the old armchair opposite Mrs Johnson. 'There was no smoke in the trachea. I was not at the post-mortem but I read the report.'

Mrs Johnson nodded and bowed her head, as if in prayer.

Yellich allowed a few moments of silence to pass before he asked, 'Do you know of anyone who would want to harm Mrs Dent, your sister?'

'Harm Muriel?' Mrs Johnson seemed shocked. 'Heavens, no. Why would you think that?'

'We don't think it, it's a possibility that we have to explore. We believe that your sister and her husband were murdered.'

'Murdered...' Mrs Johnson sank backwards. 'That word...never in my born days did I think that this family would be visited by murder...It is...it is like a stain that can't be removed. My Nigel, Mr Johnson, he succumbed to natural causes, there is no shame in that, but to have one of yours murdered...'

'Well, there is not necessarily any shame in the other. It happens all the time...sadly.'

'But natural causes, that is God's will. Murder can be prevented...'

How? thought Yellich. Please, please, please tell us how and we'll all sleep safer. But he kept his own counsel. Then he asked again, 'Was anybody threatening Mrs Dent, that you know of?'

'Not that I know of...Mr Dent, Anthony, he was the businessman, he'd have enemies, you would have thought.'

'That is an obvious avenue and is being explored, but it appears that Mr and Mrs Dent were murdered at the same time. There was an attempt to dispose of the bodies...there was a motivation to murder them. If Mr Dent wasn't the target, then perhaps Mrs Dent, for some reason as yet unknown, might have been.'

'I see...I see...I can understand that way of thinking but I can assure you, Mr...'

'Yellich.'

'Yellich...a strange name. Quite pleasant but strange.'

'East European, we think, possibly a corruption of another name, lost in the mists of time.'

'Ah...but no...I cannot see Muriel making an enemy either in her private life or her professional life. She and Anthony were private people, had few friends but they liked it that way. She just didn't socialise enough to make enemies and an accountant doesn't make enemies...If a client is over-taxed the money is refunded and the tax-man, the Inland Revenue, likes accountants because they speak the same language, they play within the rules. The Revenue doesn't want to cheat the taxpayer; the accountant doesn't help the taxpayer cheat the Revenue. So I can't see an accountant making an enemy of anyone.'

'Fair point.' Yellich nodded.

'I'd look closer to home if I were you.'

'Meaning?'

'Their children...those two...particularly

that Gregory.'

'*That* Gregory,' Yellich echoed the phrase. 'You don't sound as though you like him.'

'I don't. I never did and I never will. I have to say that our parents...that is, Muriel and my parents...'

'Yes?'

'Our parents were more supportive of the notion of adopting than we believe Anthony's parents were. I think they realized Muriel's need to be a mother, even an adoptive mother...but I don't like Gregory. His eyes...there was a look in his eyes, as though he was laughing at the world around him ...and that's when he was just seven. The look in his eyes was, and still is, one of evil. Juliette less so, though I did detect a vicious streak in her on occasions but Juliette's problem when she was growing up was that she was easily led by her brother. Now she's away from his influence and has a good marriage, well, things are better for her...but when she was a girl, if ever she misbehaved it was because Gregory would have put her up to it. One moment and I'll show you what I mean.' Mabel Johnson levered herself up from the armchair with some difficulty.

'Don't need one of those spring buttoned chairs yet,' she joked, 'not yet.' Once on her feet she walked out of the room and seemed to Yellich to be able to manage the stairs with ease and he heard her rummaging about the room directly above the room in which he sat.

He waited. Once again he glanced round the room. Neat, tidy and clean, little to soften the room, he thought, a television set in the corner on a polished table with a lower level on which lay the *Radio Times*. Other than that, he saw no sign of any recreation in the room; no magazines, no books...just the television. The room was clean, no dust that he could detect, the green three-piece suite seemed to clash with the blue of the carpet but one person's taste is not another's, and the mirror on the wall above the mantelpiece seemed to be from an earlier era, as did the wood-encased clock which stood directly beneath the mirror. Outside a milk float rattled and whined by.

Mrs Johnson descended the stairs and stood in the doorway of the room. 'Shall we sit in the kitchen?' She held a cardboard shoebox under her arm. 'It's easier to do this in the kitchen.'

The kitchen was long and thin with yellow coloured wall cupboards and work surfaces. Definitely of an earlier era, 1960s thought Yellich. Against one wall of the kitchen was a table with a matching yellow Formica surface with a metal framed upright chair at either end. Mrs Johnson sat at the further end, by the back door of the house, Yellich sat in the second chair opposite the gas cooker. There was no fridge. Quite remarkable, he thought, to encounter a household in Britain in the early twenty-first century that does not appear to have a refrigerator. It was as if the entire house was in a time warp, as if the Johnsons had moved in when newly married, decorated it and had then been content to grow old. The bathroom, he felt, was sure to have porcelain ducks flying across the wall.

'It's in this lot.' Mrs Johnson pulled the top off the cardboard box and revealed the contents to be an assortment of photographic prints, mostly colour, but some in black and white.

'Really?' Yellich began to protest, knowing that police time is valuable time.

'No...I want you to see this.' Mrs Johnson's long, bony fingers began to claw through the photographs. 'One day I am going to write on the back of these...you know, what each one is, where it is, that sort of thing. I will do it...one day...but this won't take long because I know what the photograph looks like, it's larger and it's black and white. Black and white prints work better sometimes, Mr Johnson said, and he used to be a very keen photographer. Many of his photographs are upstairs in albums; these are just snaps I took with my little camera. Now...ah, here we are.' She handed Yellich a black and white photograph. 'We had a day trip to the coast. That's our family as it was shortly after Gregory and Juliette joined us. That's one...you'll recognize it, I'm sure.'

'North Bay promenade, Scarborough.'

'Yes, it's as easily recognized by people in the north east of England as Brighton Pavilion is by folk in the south. Don't like the south of England. I feel as though I am cheating when I am down there...life's too soft...but yes, that's where it is. The Corner Café as it used to be to the left...I took this snap.'

Yellich looked at the photograph, two men and a woman grinned at the camera, between them were a small boy and a small girl and Yellich saw then what Mabel Johnson meant. The girl, the young Juliette, held a bucket and spade and smiled sheepishly at the camera. There was, thought Yellich, an appealing sincerity about her, but the boy's eyes...the look therein chilled him. 'This is young Gregory?'

'Yes...see what I mean? Those eyes...'

'Yes...yes, I do.' Yellich pondered the facial expression of young Gregory. He was smiling as clearly asked by the photographer, but the smile... his smile of all the five smiles was transparently insincere. His eyes had a gleam about them, like a predator sensing an easy kill, it was as though the photographer amused him, as though he was not smiling for the camera, but rather laughing at it, as though he was looking down with huge condescension at Mrs Johnson and her 'little camera' and that, at the age of seven years. 'Yes...I do, I really do see what you mean. Not healthy at all.'

'That is what they brought into our family.

We were only ever aunt and uncle; we didn't want to get any closer. I didn't see my sister as much as I would have liked, especially during the holiday times. We did visit when they had packed him off to boarding school, but not as often as I would have liked. We felt frightened of him...myself and Mr Johnson...we both said as much...didn't want to let him get close enough to damage us. You'll have heard about the dog?'

'The dog?'

'The old Labrador that died shortly after Gregory and Juliette joined the family. He was an old dog but had some years yet. Big Tom took an instant dislike to Gregory and was found curled up one day in the small wood by the house. No damage...no injuries ...just lying dead. Could have been natural, of course. Juliette was upset by the old dog's death, but Gregory wasn't...seemed quite pleased, so Muriel told me.'

'Well, my boss is chatting to Mr Dent's brother now.'

'The motorcyclist?'

'I believe so...yes.'

'Well, he'll tell your boss the same story. Doubtless he'll tell him about the cats as well.'

'The cats?'

'They disappeared...four of them over time...but once Gregory had been given a shotgun to play with...'

'A shotgun! To play with!'

'Well...to play with is my expression. It was a small bore gun...a 410 I think they are called.'

'Yes.'

'To keep vermin down, a job they thought he might enjoy, to control him, to bring him into the fold. He was a teenager by then... mid to late teens...and then the four cats disappeared over a period of as many months. I am sure Robin will have told your boss about that.'

'I am sure he will have done.' Yellich stood and handed the photograph back to Mrs Johnson. 'I am sure he will have done. Thank you, this has been illuminating.'

It was Tuesday, 10.30 a.m.

Hennessey handed Yellich the file. 'I've met the type before.'

Yellich read the file, then closed it and said, 'So have I. Not guilty despite overwhelming evidence. We meet them all the time. I can never fathom their minds. What do you think we should do? Pull him in for a quiz session?'

Hennessey drew breath between his teeth. 'Don't know ... don't know.' He glanced to his side, looked out of his office window at the stone battlements of the ancient city. He thought how cold they looked, sharply angular under a low, grey sky. Perhaps they looked that way, he further thought, because it was that time of the year, that run up to Christmas deeply felt by him in Jennifer's absence. Still after all these years. Though he had people to buy for: a son, daughter-in-law, grandchildren...and one significant other. Soon it would be time to send Christmas cards, not too early so as to seem needy nor too late to give the impression that the card was an afterthought. He sent about forty, and received the same number – not bad; he was as integrated as he wanted to be. He hadn't the emotional energy to be universally popular and jealously guarded his free time and his solitude and loved the evening walk with Oscar as much as Oscar appeared to relish it. He turned again to face Yellich who sat patiently waiting for Hennessey's response. 'Don't know,' he said again. 'The boy is clever, I don't want to start him... don't want to give him any inkling that he is under suspicion until we have proof positive.'

'If we get it!' Yellich raised an eyebrow.

'Yes...yes, you're right...we won't get a confession.' He tapped the file. 'Not if this is anything to go by. His prints all over the safe, and the window where he broke into the office, the money, all of it, found in his van at the site and he pleads not guilty because it was his money to steal. Have you ever heard the like?'

'Yes...' Yellich laughed, 'as we have said many times, "Have we heard the like?"'

Hennessey grinned. 'Point to you.' He paused, glancing in the opposite direction at the police mutual calendar on the wall, the open door into the CID corridor. 'I think we need more on this fella.'

'More, sir?'

'More. I mean...I have told you what Robin Dent told me, and you have told me what Mabel Johnson told you. Pretty much the same message, pretty much the same sort of impression. I would like to see the photograph you describe, the dog that died, the cats that disappeared, stealing money, which through some twisted rationalization he believed was his. Three thousand pounds in the safe but he only took two thousand because that was what he believed was owed to him when in fact he wasn't owed a penny. He was employed on a fixed salary and wasn't entitled to directors' fees like his adoptive father and mother, so he broke in and took them anyway but left one thousand to show how honest he is...or was. We'll have better luck nailing this Johnny the more we know about him.'

'What do you suggest, boss?'

'A trip to East Hull.' Hennessey glanced at his watch. 'Midday...take an hour to get there...So we'll eat like the weary foot soldiers we are, then drive out to the children's home he was in for a brief period. The staff will have changed by now but we might be able to pick a moved on or retired brain or two. What are you doing for lunch?'

'Canteen, skipper.'

'Ugh...don't know how you can stand that stodge.'

'It's cheap.' Yellich stood. 'My wallet likes it very well.'

'Alright, meet here in about an hour, then we'll drive to Hull. Not my favourite city...'

Hennessey cloaked himself against the north-east 'biter' in coat, hat and scarf, signed out and left Micklegate Bar police station and chose to walk down Micklegate itself, assuming that his usual route, upon the walls, would still be too exposed and Micklegate, he reasoned, was not an unattractive uphill and then downhill walk. The narrow street, within the walls, had buildings that interested him, such as the ancient terraced houses on Priory Street, with their narrow frontage and far reaching floor space, the ancient churches and graveyards and the pubs. So, so many pubs, that have given rise to the 'Micklegate challenge' or 'the walk'. One must start at Micklegate Bar, and stop at each pub and have one half pint of beer, then move on to the next pub for another half pint of beer. So far no one, not even the most hardened drinker has made it to Bridge Street at the further end of Micklegate.

But this is York, Hennessey mused; at least

the old city, the city within the walls. Shops in Micklegate sang forth Christmas with lights and greetings, although it was not until Hennessey had crossed the Ouse that he met the full onslaught of the season, where lights were strung across the street, and attached to lamp posts, where the streets and the pedestrian precinct were thronged, even at midweek, with shoppers carrying bulging bags, not, he found, with a look of joy, but with a look of single-minded determination. His Christmas was going to be low-key, but at least it would be very inexpensive. The principal gift he would be buying for his household, for example, was a leg of lamb to be roasted for Oscar's Christmas dinner. He walked down Coney Street to St Leonard's Square where street musicians playing whistles (badly) competed with a Salvation Army band whose brass renderings of the old favourite carols Hennessey thought faultless. He was not trained in musical appreciation but he stood a while and listened to 'Hark, the Herald Angels Sing' and 'God Rest Ye Merry, Gentlemen'. Turning into the wind, he walked into Stonegate and then left into an alleyway at the end of which narrow covered passage was the entrance to Ye Olde Starre Inn, York's oldest pub. Being of festive mood, Hennessey ordered roast turkey, roast potatoes and stuffing which he relished whilst sitting in a quiet corner beneath a framed print of a map showing 'The West Ridinge of Yorkshyrre, the moft famous and faire Citie Yorke, defcribed – 1610'. Replenished, Hennessey retraced his steps to Micklegate Bar police station. He found Yellich sitting at his desk reading the *Yorkshire Post*. 'Ready?'

'As I'll ever be.' Yellich folded the paper and laid it on his desk. He reached for his coat and hat. 'Want me to drive, boss?'

'If you would.' Hennessey turned. 'If you would...you know I prefer not to.'

Hennessey always experienced the same sensations when visiting the city of Kingston upon Hull, on Humber's muddy northern bank, dissected by its own equally muddy river. He sensed that he was going down into something. It was all there: the folk were the same; the traffic drove on the same side of the road as in the rest of the kingdom; the large department stores had the same names as the chains in other towns and cities, yet...yet...he always felt that there was something missing in respect of the city.

The man was friendly, warm, affable. 'It was a children's home,' he said, smiling with large eyes, 'but that's old hat now...all is down to fostering children in the community. The move away from institutional care started a long time ago. We still have a few homes but not as many as before and Sycamore Lodge stopped being a children's home many years ago.'

Upon entering Hull down Anlaby Road, past the hospital, turning left at the railway station, Yellich had then forged his way east through the city and by enquiring at post offices and estate agents, managed to find Sycamore Lodge on Swallow Road. The building was clearly Victorian and, in Hennessey's eyes, was a monstrosity of complicated lines and turrets and dormer windows that interrupted the roof line. The building of red brick seemed to squat heavily on the ground it occupied. The door was opened by a pale skinned youth of about sixteen years who spoke in monosyllables but eventually directed Hennessey and Yellich to 'the chief's' office. The interior of the building Hennessey found to be as complex as the exterior as he and Yellich followed the youth's directions down twisting, undulating corridors until they came to a door with a sign reading 'The Chief' pinned with a single drawing pin. Hennessey tapped on the door and a jocular voice said, 'Come in.' 'The chief' revealed himself to be a man of middle years, Afro-Caribbean, and warmly told Hennessey that children's homes were 'old hat'.

'These youths are school leavers,' he explained. 'Unemployed. In some cases already unemployable. This is a drop-in centre. We teach what we can: social skills, interview skills, but when we shut up for the day, they go home. It's non residential. The youths are here because it's better for them to be here than wandering the streets. It's too easy to get heroin and crack in Hull. We do that as well, advise about drugs, the dangers therein. We get ex-addicts to talk to them about life in the gutter. So, how can I help you? Your warrant card said York. One of our lads or lassies got their prints in York?'

'Possibly...but we are here looking to pick brains.'

'Won't find many of those round here... staff or users,' the man said as he smiled. 'I'm Payper by the way.'

'Paper?'

'Sam Payper.' The chief smiled. 'Pronounced like newspaper but spelled with a *y*.'

'Ah...I see...well, we need to speak to someone who worked at Sycamore Lodge when it was an old hat children's home. This is our first port of call.'

'Oh...I see.'

'About twenty years ago, probably a little more.'

'Again, I see. I think the only way to do that is to pick up networks.' He turned and reached for the telephone. He picked it up and dialled a six-figure number from memory. 'The building is still owned and run by Social Services,' he said as he dialled. 'Hull is one of those departments, unlike London boroughs, where people stay, move on within the department but stay. This fella will be the one to ask.' He waited. 'Not at his desk.

Oh...Harold. Hello, Sam Payper. Listen, I have two gentlemen with me from the bold constabulary of York. Yes...indeed.' Sam Payper turned and winked at Hennessey. 'Yes, they are keen to pick brains.' Payper laughed. 'Yes, that's what I said too but they are keen to interview someone, anyone who worked at Sycamore Lodge when it was a children's home, about twenty years ago.' Payper listened then turned to Hennessey and asked, 'What specifically is your inquiry about? It could help track down the right brains for you to pick. Are you trying to trace a member of staff...or one of the children?'

'We want to find someone who recalls two children by the name of Gregory and Juliette Locke.' Hennessey saw no reason not to inform the helpful Sam Payper of their purpose. 'Brother and sister...came into care as orphans following a road traffic accident in which their parents were killed.'

'I see.'

'Left care when they were adopted by Mr and Mrs Dent, of Great Sheldwich, Vale of York.'

'Right.' Sam Payper spoke into the phone,

146

relaying the information Hennessey had provided. Then he turned to Hennessey and said, 'I can hear them asking for you. As I said, it's just one of those departments...you work your way into the bricks. Ah...you've got a result? Perhaps...yes...hello...right, got that.' He scribbled on a sheet of paper then said, 'Thanks,' and replaced the receiver. He turned to Hennessey. 'Got a paper and pen?' Yellich reached into his pocket and extracted his notebook and ballpoint.

'OK.' Sam Payper leaned forward. 'Ada Beadnall was the officer in charge of Sycamore Lodge when it was a children's home. She has retired to the coast. There's quite a lot of land between Hull and the east coast even though Hull is a seaport. She lives out by Withernsea. They are phoning her at home right now to see if they can let you have her address. She may in fact phone here. I am sure she will be very curious... that will make her eager to help. I know I would if I were retired. It's all behind you, then you have a part to play again. The other one is Alex Davies...I know him...he's a good bloke. He started out in social work as an unqualified member of staff straight from university working here, then did the training course and is now a middle manager with the Fostering and Adoption section.' Sam Payper tapped the paper he held in his hand. 'You know, he could be useful, he could fast track access to the file on those two orphans, they'll still be in the archives.'

'That,' said Hennessey, 'that would be very useful, very useful indeed.'

The phone rang. Sam Payper smiled. 'This will be Ada Beadnall.' He looked at the phone. 'Do you not think the ring has an insistent quality?' He picked up the phone. 'Sycamore Lodge,' he said. 'Yes...just here.' He handed the phone to Hennessey. 'Miss Beadnall, for you.'

Hennessey took the phone and indicated to Yellich that he wanted to use the notepad and pen. Yellich handed them to him and watched as Hennessey held the phone to his ear with one hand and scribbled with the other. Eventually he thanked the caller very much and replaced the handset. 'You were right.' He smiled at Sam Payper. 'She is very eager to help. She is at home at the moment.' He glanced at his watch. 'We don't have the time to visit both by the two of us so...' He handed Yellich his notepad. 'That is Miss Beadnall's address. Can you drive out and visit her?'

'Yes, skipper.'

'See what she can tell you about Gregory and Juliette Locke, as they were.' Hennessey turned to Sam Payper. 'Who did you say the other chap was?'

'Alex...Alex Davies. He works in the centre of the city. I can run you there.'

'Could you?'

'Of course.' Sam Payper picked up the phone and dialled a number. When it was answered he asked for Alex Davies in Fostering and Adoption, then he handed the phone to Hennessey. 'Suggest you make a courtesy call,' he said. 'Let him know you're about to call on him and why.'

Having arranged to rendezvous with Hennessey at the cafeteria in the once grandly named Hull Paragon Railway Station, and by then the more modestly named Hull Railway Station, Yellich drove out to Withernsea. The wind drove keenly off the North Sea and bit into Yellich's cheeks as he got out of the car and walked up the steps of the house, being the address Hennessey had scribbled on his notepad. The house was an imposing four-storeyed terraced house that faced the sea, which was then choppy and grey. He rang the bell and waited. The door was opened with a flourish by a small, finely boned lady who Yellich thought was in her mid-sixties. She had short, grey hair and a ready smile. She moved with confidence and seemed thus far to have escaped any ravages of rheumatism or arthritis. 'Police?'

'Yes.' Yellich nodded gently and showed her his ID.

'Ah... please come in.' Ada Beadnall stepped to one side and shut the door hurriedly behind him. 'Shut the wind out,' she said. 'I love living at the coast but the easterlies in the winter...they've got teeth.'

'So I feel.' Yellich smiled. Towering over her, he felt very protective towards Miss Beadnall.

'Please...shall we sit in here?' She led him to a living room with high ceilings that looked out over the North Sea. 'You'll have tea? Please...I get so few visitors.'

'Well, thank you, yes.'

'Please take a seat.'

Yellich did so. He found the room cluttered but in a neat and managed manner, as if the room was controlled by a woman who encouraged growth and fulfilment of potential. When tea arrived it was in a generous white pot, accompanied by a tray of toasted teacakes spread with paté.

'My...' Yellich said. 'Really, this is too generous.'

'Keep the cold out. Food is the best central heating system the body can have. Are you wearing your thermals, young man? Weather like this...'

'No. If I lived here then I would, but I live in York, it's a little more sheltered there. Still a bit windy but nothing compared to Withernsea.'

'Yes...it's lovely in the summer.' She poured the tea. 'A walk along the beach in the very early morning...but you pay for it in the winter.' She handed Yellich a cup of tea. 'Do help yourself to a teacake. So...on the phone you said it was about Gregory and Juliette Locke?'

'Well, that wasn't me, it was my boss, but yes...we are interested in anything you can tell us.'

'Why? Are they in trouble?'

'Possibly...I'd rather not say too much just yet.'

'Well...' Ada Beadnall poured herself a cup of tea and sat back in her chair. 'My sister was a teacher, she is retired now, and she says that looking back over the years she remembers the good ones and the bad ones ...the others just...well, failed to impress upon her memory. In social work it's pretty much the same and I remember the Locke children very well.'

'Good or bad?'

'Bad, very bad, particularly Gregory. Those eyes...large brown...so menacing, wouldn't let you get past them...just couldn't see his soul. I remember once we took in an arsonist.'

'An arsonist?'

'Yes...a boy who was then older than Gregory. He had absconded from another local authority's care and had been picked up by the police. They brought him to us and we kept him for a few hours whilst his social worker made arrangements to come and pick him up. In the telephone conversation with her it was clear that she thought we were a secure unit.'

'Secure?'

'The children were kept locked up.'

'Ah...'

'When she realized that we were non secure she gasped and told us to have him transferred to a secure unit without delay. He was fourteen and had multiple convictions for arson, but I remember him because his eyes were exactly like Gregory Locke's eyes and also...frightening...Gregory and that boy just gravitated to each other, even despite the age gap. They recognized each other as kindred spirits.'

'Chilling.'

'It was very, but Gregory never actually did anything wrong or criminal. He was only seven anyway, but he just seemed to slide through each day without any bad behaviour that would have enabled the staff to get hold of his personality. We just could not make an assessment of that boy. I remember him well...one of the bad ones who never misbehaved, yet when he was in there, other children misbehaved in a way that was very out of character. Then after they had found a home with that couple in York and were discharged from our care, things just settled down again...back to normal. Staff commented on it. How we seemed to have been visited by someone or something that created a lot of trouble but never could be blamed for anything, as if the other children were responding to his personality...or were receiving messages from him that the staff were unaware of.'

'Messages?'

'On a psychological level...as if without actually saying anything, he was manipulating them.'

'I see. What was his sister like?'

'Healthier. She misbehaved but I and the staff always had the impression she was very easily led by him.'

'Interesting.'

'Very...like I said, you only remember the good ones and the bad ones and I remember Gregory Locke. I'll tell you something else as well...they were orphaned, recently orphaned, but you wouldn't have thought it. No emotion, no grief, no distress, not from him. She was a little more timid but he just stepped over the threshold and cast his eyes about the building as though he was assuming occupation and control...at seven years of age. Do have another teacake.'

Hennessey thought Alexander Davies to be a sorrowful looking man. He was, thought Hennessey, a man in his mid-forties. He seemed to have made a perfunctory attempt at being 'office smart' but the unironed blue shirt which ill matched the loud red tie told of a man whose mind was elsewhere. His office was untidy, though in Hennessey's experience that meant little. In his capacity as a police officer he had visited many Departments of Social Work and in the course of doing so had learned that a tidy desk therein was something of a rarity. Alex Davies cast a glance at a photograph of a woman with two adult children which stood on the windowsill of his office. 'The Locke children?'
'Yes.'
'I actually remember them being admitted, but I left Sycamore Lodge shortly afterwards, went to Sheffield University for professional training. Big mistake, should have gone to sea like my father on the

trawlers, got my ticket. I would have been a skipper by now. The fishing can be danger- ous, but it's not as soul sapping as this game.' He slapped his desk. 'Anyway, I have sent down to the archives for the file on the Locke children. It'll take some digging out but I phoned the request as soon as I re- ceived your call.' He glanced at his watch. 'Should be here by now. Sorry...sorry...I am not really myself; I have just lost my wife you see.'

'Oh...I am sorry.'

'Yes...she was only forty-two, breast can- cer...she was so brave.'

Hennessey smiled. He allowed Davies to see his smile.

'You smile at my misfortune, Mr Hennes- sey?' Davies's voice had an angry edge.

'No...no...I wouldn't do that. No, I smile because I am a sputnik.'

'A sputnik? A satellite? What do you mean?'

'Sputnik is a Russian word, it means fel- low traveller.'

'I didn't know that.'

'Take it from me...it's an inspired name for a satellite travelling with planet earth through space.'

'Isn't it just?'

'Well, I too am a widower...I know what you are feeling, but you had a good marriage, your wife saw your children grow.'

'Only twenty years...and she didn't see them complete university and settle down.'

'Well, we were married for barely two years,' Hennessey said, 'and Jennifer died when our son was just six months old.'

Alex Davies put his hand to his mouth. 'I am so sorry, I must sound so selfish.'

'Don't worry...she'll never die in a sense, if you keep your memory alive.'

'Oh, I will.' He glanced at the photograph. 'What happened to your wife, if I might ask?'

'Natural causes too...in her case it was Sudden Death Syndrome.'

'I have heard of that, strikes young, very healthy people, life just leaves them...no one knows the medical cause.'

'Yes, that's it...Jennifer was walking through Easingwold, where I still live in the same house, it was a hot day, folk thought she had fainted and called an ambulance, but she was dead on arrival...twenty-three years old.'

'Oh...'

'I scattered her ashes in the garden then spent the next few years landscaping the garden to her design. One of the last things she did was to design the garden. It was as flat and as dull as a football pitch when we bought the house, now it has orchards and ponds with thriving pond life.'

'Sounds very nice.' Davies smiled gently.

'I will not move...I talk to her each day. I return home and tell her of my day. An observer would think I was talking to myself, but I sense her presence...I really do. I have a significant other in my life, a divorced lady, a recent development which delights me...told Jennifer of her and just know she approves.'

'That is the attitude. You've given me something there, Mr Hennessey, thank you. Chloe would want me to pick up and carry on...find someone else in time, but I will always treasure her memory.'

'I am sure you will.'

There was a tap on Alex Davies' office door. It was opened without further invitation and a nervous looking bespectacled girl in a yellow dress advanced on Davies' desk and handed him a manila file. 'I was asked to bring this to you, Mr Davies,' she stammered.

'Ah...thank you.' Davies smiled as he took hold of the file. 'I appreciate it.'

The young woman quickly withdrew, leaving Hennessey and Davies alone again.

'I might not be able to let you look at this, not without a warrant...they are strictly confidential, you see.'

'Then why bring it out of the archive? I am sure I'll be able to obtain a warrant but I could have saved a journey if I had known I would need one.'

'Well, it depends on what you want. I might be able to let you have some information but not all. Information about their adoptive parents, for example, that would need a warrant.'

'Ah...I am not interested in them. What can you tell me about the Locke children?'

'We'll see.' Davies opened the file. 'Parents Richard and Linda Locke, died in a car accident...known to you.'

'Really?'

'Yes, there's a pre-sentence report from

the probation service here, receiving stolen goods. I can let you have a look at that.' Davies took the report from the file and handed it to Hennessey. 'A career criminal by the look of that track.'

'Seems so...receiving...receiving...fraud... embezzlment. He did a bit of time...he was inside when...yes, when both his children were born...nothing violent, though.' Hennessey scanned the report. 'I do believe that violence leads to more violence but nothing here to indicate that Gregory Locke's early life was violent.'

'It is Gregory whom the police are interested in?'

'Yes...can't tell you why, but yes. Not a good role model but Gregory's father doesn't come across as a violent person.'

'Well, you don't have to hit someone to be violent.' Davies leaned forward and folded his arms, resting them on his desk. 'You can be violent in your attitude, in your speech, and I still remain struck by how indifferent to his parents' death did young Gregory Locke seem. Very detached, emotionally speaking. Some damage was done to him, some considerable damage – which is to explain his attitude, not to excuse it.'

'Yes...' Hennessey growled, though he was surprised to find that Davies as a social worker was not what he privately referred to as an 'abuse excuse merchant'. 'His mother was no saint either...she had a few convictions. It's referred to here...a joint prosecution for fraud.'

'Crimes of a devious nature, unlike more honest crimes like assault, if you see what I mean? The crimes here seem to be entered into with the intention of not merely getting away with it, but of avoiding all suspicion in the first place. If he grew up in that devious sort of household it would rub off on him, he would become a devious adult.'

'But not violent?'

'I would say not but then I am not a psychologist.'

'Near enough,' Hennessey smiled. 'But this has been interesting...if only in that it points to the possible elimination of our prime suspect. Possibly.'

It was Tuesday, 16.30 hours.

Five

Wednesday, December 17,
10.25 hours – 14.30 hours
*in which the investigation becomes
greatly confused.*

The red recording light glowed, the twin
cassettes of the tape recorder spun slowly.

'The time is 10.25 a.m., the date is the
seventeenth of December. The place is Interview Room Two, Micklegate Bar Police
Station, York. I am Detective Chief Inspector Hennessey. I am now going to ask the
other people in the room to identify themselves.'

'Detective Sergeant Yellich.'

'Ambrose Peebles, of Ellis, Burden, Woodland and Lake, solicitors, attending in
accordance with the Police and Criminal
Evidence Act 1985.' Peebles spoke confi-

dently, softly, with, thought Hennessey, perfectly enunciated received pronunciation.

'Gregory Dent.' Dent spoke curtly, he smiled slightly, his eyes had that reported glassy look, Hennessey noted, preventing anyone seeing into them, to assess his soul.

'Mr Dent,' Hennessey began, 'you have been brought to the police station in connection with the murder of your adoptive parents, Anthony and Muriel Dent.'

'I have?' Dent smirked.

'You have. You are under suspicion.'

'Of...?'

'Murder.'

'Really?' Dent sat forward, smiling confidently.

'You have the motivation. Has your parents' will been read?'

'Where there's a will, there's a way, is that what you are saying?'

'If you'd just answer the question.'

'Yes, it has. I am a rich man now. I intend to visit the Porsche dealership at my earliest convenience.'

'What have you inherited?'

'Quite a lot...enough to see me out without doing a stroke of work for the rest of my life, if I am shrewd in my investments.'

'What did the will say?'

'Well, my sister and I inherit pretty much everything: the house at Great Sheldwich, the farmland that adjoins it, the business premises at Precenters Court, the caravan site and all those caravans, the other plots of land here and there, the car parks on the prime building land. If we can get planning permission for a hotel on the caravan site ...Juliette and I talked about it last night. Neither of us wants to carry on with any of the businesses, though we might keep a couple of the car parks as a safety net, one each, to let some income trickle in, but we are going to liquidize the rest. I'm going south; London's the place for a young man with my sort of money.'

'Young man with your sort of money? You could not wait until your parents died of natural causes by which time you'd be middle aged.'

'Mr Hennessey,' Ambrose Peebles growled. He was a well-set man, in his fifties, expensively dressed in silk shirt and quality three-piece suit. 'I must protest. Do you have any evidence with which you can support your suspicions?'

'No,' Dent replied, holding eye contact with Hennessey. 'No, he hasn't because there is none to be had. I have a cast-iron alibi for the night of the murders. My girl-friend told me you had visited her. She has confirmed my alibi for you.' Dent paused. 'All the time you are wasting on me is the time you could be devoting to appre-hending the actual culprit. They were my parents...I have clear recollections of my real parents, I was seven when they died, but the Dents brought me up, paid for my education, took me into the family business. I want their murderer caught and brought to justice.'

'They didn't take you as far into the business as you would have liked, did they? A management position at the caravan site was as far "in" as you were allowed, and from which you stole.'

Dent's face hardened. A look of anger flashed across his eyes.

'Yes, we know about that...we have done some checking.'

'Shows how honest I am,' Dent said shrug-ging. 'Technically a crime...but morally, not so. You see I should have got director's fees as well.'

'But you were not a director. You were employed.'

'I was a member of the family. My parents got directors' fees of £2,000 after a period of trading. I was their son; I should have got the same, so I took it. There was £3,000 in the safe but I only took the £2,000 owed to me. Honest man.'

'The police charged you, the magistrates convicted you; they clearly didn't see you as an honest man. They saw you as a thief.'

'They were wrong. I took what was mine. If I was a thief, I would have taken the whole 3K.'

'Your parents were in your way. You got rid of them.'

'Oh yes? How? I was with Susan...'

'Just the two of you?'

'Yes.'

'Any independent witnesses?'

'No, I was with her, she was with me...we spent the evening alone.'

'But no one can verify that?'

'No.'

Hennessey paused. Then he asked, 'So,

what happened to the cats?'

'The cats?'

'The cats belonging to the Dents, they disappeared over a period of a few months, coincidental it seemed with your taking the 410 to shoot vermin. And the dog that died shortly after you arrived at West End House, the dog that took an instant dislike to you. What did you do to him, you, aged seven years?'

Ambrose Peebles glanced at Hennessey. 'Really, Inspector, you have no evidence at all. A dog that died over twenty years ago...I mean...really...you are not just clutching at straws, you are grasping at thin air. I am not impressed.'

'Do we need to talk to Mrs Thurnham?'

'Dare say you can if you like...doubt she can tell you anything.'

'You are providing false alibis for each other, you're both implicated in the murders of the Dents.'

Gregory Dent smirked. 'That is preposterous. Susan has no motivation in the murders.'

'She'd share in your money.'

'That wouldn't be at all guaranteed. Possibly, possibly, if we were married, and she could expect some share of the money or a claim on it if we divorced...then, yes... perhaps, perhaps then...but as a mere girl-friend, even a promise of a share of any inheritance would be meaningless...can't enforce that.'

'Inspector,' Ambrose Peebles spoke softly, 'this is going nowhere. I must ask you to either charge my client with some offence or other, or release him.'

'Very well.' Hennessey reached for the stop button. 'This interview is terminated at 11.15 hours.' He pressed the stop button. 'Sergeant, will you please escort these two gentlemen to the door?'

Ten minutes later, in Hennessey's office, Hennessey said, 'He is up to his neck in those murders, Yellich, I can feel it...I feel it in my waters.'

'Probably, sir, but his brief is right, you'll need more than your waters to be able to nail him, and maybe the real culprit is out there...maybe we are not just barking up the wrong tree, we are in the wrong part of the forest.'

'Oh, you're right, you're right...the culprit

is out there. He left five minutes ago on his way to the Porsche dealership. How much do you think he is worth?'

Yellich shook his head. He glanced out of the window of Hennessey's office; rain was falling vertically from a low, grey sky, causing the ancient walls to shine. 'Well, he has to split it with his sister, but he could realize eight figures if he liquidated, I'd say.'

'I'd say so too.' Hennessey stared ahead with a look of grim determination. 'That's one million reasons to murder his parents.'

'Don't close your mind too early, boss.'

'I'm not. That man is evil...I will be proved right.'

The phone on his desk rang, he snatched it up and Yellich watched as the colour drained from Hennessey's face. Hennessey listened and then mumbled his thanks and replaced the handset. 'There's been another.'

'Another, skipper?'

'Body...burned...charred...found just now ...our attendance is requested.'

'Good old dog walkers.' The uniformed sergeant talked with a resigned attitude, as though he had seen it many times before. He was an elderly sergeant, close to retirement, Hennessey judged. He had a life-hardened look across his eyes and Hennessey thought that it would take much to make him smile. 'They find most of them. I tell you, sir, if it wasn't for dog walkers, a lot of bodies would never be found. Dog walkers, hikers...hikers too, but mainly dog walkers.'

Hennessey looked at the corpse, a male he thought, but he found it difficult to tell. It was face down with the chest raised off the ground as the arms and legs had contracted as the body burned. There was little else he could do, but view the corpse, as if by doing so he triggered the investigation process in his mind; it made the crime 'real' for him. He nodded and stepped outside the inflatable tent that had been erected over the body. The dour, humourless sergeant followed him. There was no need for a police presence inside the tent. The two men walked from the tent and ducked beneath the blue and white police tape which had been strung around the crime scene. He approached Yellich. 'Want to see it?'

'Not particularly, boss. I assume it is just like the other two and there will be photographs for me to study.'

Hennessey turned his collar up against the wind which blew from the east finding its way easily between the swaying trees of the small wood in which the charred body was found. 'Aye,' he muttered. 'It is just like the others, burned and blackened, burned to a crisp, dumped too, just like the others. No sign of burning on the vegetation and it was dumped next to a gorse bush. Ever seen a gorse bush burn?'

'Confess I haven't.'

'Terrifying, you'd think the plant was made of petrol. Had he been burned here, that plant would definitely have gone up in flames...So, dumped...like the others.' He turned to the uniformed sergeant. 'Anything of note?'

'I think there is...yes, sir. I'll show you.'

'Stay here and wait for Dr D'Acre please, Yellich, she's on her way.'

'Yes, boss.' Yellich thrust his hands into his coat pockets and stamped his feet. 'Damn cold,' he said, more to himself than to Hennessey.

'Walk about.' Hennessey smiled. 'But so long as you remain in the vicinity of the tent...the police have to welcome the forensic pathologist.'

'Understood, sir.'

'OK, sergeant, what have you got?'

The sergeant led Hennessey along a pathway to the edge of the wood beyond which was a road, a narrow badly surfaced road, and beyond the road were winter brown ploughed fields and hedgerows, and beyond them the low skyline of the city of York. Between the wood and the road was a shallow stream, really no more than a trickle of water. A constable stood by the stream. He stiffened as Hennessey and the sergeant approached.

'The water has kept the ground here a bit muddy.' The sergeant stopped a little short of the stream. 'There are tyre tracks.'

'So I see.' Hennessey looked at the ground. The tyre tracks were short; very little muddy ground was to be had between the stream and the point where the soil was frozen. 'Better get Scene of Crime to photograph them.'

'Already done so, sir,' the sergeant said

dryly.

'Good man.'

'I asked them if they'd take plaster casts once you had seen them.'

'Again, thank you.' Hennessey looked at the tyre tracks. 'Nothing distinctive,' he muttered, 'not even enough to say they have anything to set them apart from any other tracks...no uneven wear for example, no damage, but we can identify the make, that's a start.'

'Better than nothing,' the sergeant growled.

'As you say.' He looked about him. 'So, the vehicle reversed off the lane, had to; the dirt from the wheels is on the road surface...see it turning away to the right?'

'That's the easiest way to York from here, sir.'

'I see. Where would a left turn take you?'

'A small village...Anslow...then eventually the A19 to Thirsk or back to York.'

'I see...Well, assuming that this vehicle did convey the corpse, we can identify the tyre make and possibly the make of vehicle. The tyre tread is narrow.'

'Yes, small vehicle alright, sir.'

'The dog walker who found the body?'

'At home, sir...in Anslow. I have her details in my notebook. I would have asked her to remain but she was very shaken.'

'I can imagine...I can well imagine. She didn't tell you anything?'

'Nothing, sir. Pointed to where we would find the body, then gave her name and address and said she was going home.'

'Alright.' He turned to the constable. 'Continue to wait here.'

'Yes, sir.'

'Once the SOCO have taken plaster casts, can you report to the sergeant? But until then remain here.'

'Yes, sir.' He was a young man, about nineteen, thought Hennessey. This was probably his first murder. Hennessey knew it wouldn't be his last.

Hennessey and the sergeant walked purposefully back over the hard ground to where the inflatable tent was erected. He saw Dr D'Acre arriving. She was tall, slender and with good muscle tone, leggy, short cropped hair, serious attitude...She walked equally purposefully towards the tent, carrying a black Gladstone bag in her right hand. She and Hennessey nodded to each other as they met.

'Another, I believe,' she said when she and Hennessey were close enough to talk without raising their voices.

'Yes.' Hennessey nodded solemnly. 'In the tent.'

'Well, I'll see what I will see. If it is like the other two there will be little I can do here.' She had, thought Hennessey, a smooth, balanced face, wore no make-up save for a trace of very pale lipstick. 'I'll be conducting the PM this afternoon. Will you be attending for the police, Chief Inspector?'

'Probably...if not myself then Sergeant Yellich. I want to go and talk to the lady who found the corpse. I should be free to attend. Sergeant...?'

'Sir?'

'If you'd see the lady pathologist to the tent?'

'Yes, sir.'

'Knew what it was as soon as I saw it.'

Hennessey had strolled into the village of Anslow and found it to be a ribbon of houses either side of the narrow road and little else, a small shop, a pub called The Bird in the Hand and a repair garage. Anslow. He opened the front gate and walked down a gravel covered path and in doing so, was reminded of a gravel covered driveway of a house in a small village just to the north of York. His feet crunching the ground caused a dog to bark from within the house. Gravel covered driveways and paths, and a metal gate that squeaks for the want of oil were, he thought, the two best burglar deterrents, save for a dog. He walked up to the door of the house, white painted, and rapped the black metal knocker. The door was opened quickly by a woman who, Hennessey thought, was in her forties. She was dark haired with a pale complexion and seemed to be large boned. An alert and well-fed springer spaniel stood at her feet barking at Hennessey. The dog was well cared for; Hennessey saw that in an instant: glossy coat, excellent muscle tone, not an ounce overweight. A lucky dog to be this woman's pet.

'You'll be the police.' The woman spoke slowly with a distinct Yorkshire accent. 'I was expecting you.'

'Yes.' Hennessey showed her his ID.

The woman nodded and stepped aside and said, 'Alright, Toby,' at which point the spaniel stopped barking and sniffed at Hennessey's legs as he entered the house. The woman shut the door behind Hennessey, closing it with a solid thud. The house was clearly very well built, probably in the 1930s, he thought. The woman led him into a sitting room which looked out on to the back garden, long, narrow and well tended.

'Please, take a seat.'

Hennessey sat and extracted his notebook from his coat pocket. 'You're Miss Eyton? Miss Paula Eyton?'

'Yes, I phoned the police. I knew what it was as soon as I saw it.'

'It is obvious...'

'Well, some folk might have had to do a double take, wait for a few seconds before fully realizing what they were looking at. But I knew immediately what it was; a charred corpse.' She paused. 'I was a firefighter for a few years. If you put out enough fires, you'll eventually put one out that has claimed lives.'

'Yes.'

'So I've seen the like before.'

'I see.' Hennessey glanced round the room. It was neat, clean. There were photographs of the dog in plentiful array, but no photograph of any human being.

'Yes...it got to me...firefighting is a highly stressed job...and I looked at the senior fire officers on parade with their bloodshot eyes...They had locked themselves away with a bottle, and I don't mean beer, slept it off...turned in for duty well the worse for wear...but it's the way they handled stress. A lot of deaths from heart attacks in the fire service, early deaths, men who died before their time...the job does that to you.'

'So I have heard.'

'Well, I got out but I took a few sights with me in my mind's eye...and charred corpses are among them. So the instant I saw it, I knew what it was. Called three nines on my mobile, waited until the boys in blue arrived, then gave my name and address and we returned home.'

'We?'

'Toby and me.' She glanced warmly at her dog. 'You can keep people. A dog gives you all you need and won't betray your trust.'

'So you take that walk daily? You and Toby?'

'Sometimes twice daily, depending on my shifts. I am a nurse.'

Hennessey smiled. 'Good for you.'

'It has its stresses but not like the fire service.'

'So the corpse appeared overnight?'

'Appeared?' Paula Eyton smiled. 'You make it sound like an apparition or as if it was conjured from thin air...but yes, it was placed where I found it some time between 4.00 p.m. yesterday and about 10.30 a.m. this forenoon.'

'Alright.' Hennessey scribbled on his pad. 'Did you see anything out of the ordinary yesterday afternoon?'

'No...smelled the body being burned, though.'

'Sorry?' Hennessey's jaw dropped. 'You smelled it being burned?'

'Yes.' Paula Eyton remained expression-less. 'Didn't realize it at the time but I smell-ed a distinct and unusual burning smell last night at about ten p.m. I didn't realize that I was smelling the corpse being burned, but putting two and two together, it must have been that that I was smelling. This is the country, farmers often have fires, burn all sorts. Fires are good things if properly used and only if properly used.'

'Yes...only if properly used,' Hennessey echoed. 'Could you tell from which direction the smell came and how far away?'

'From over there.' Paula Eyton pointed to her back garden. 'Beyond the garden there is a sort of –' she shrugged – 'I wouldn't know how to describe it. It's a hotchpotch of an area, abandoned cars, an unofficial rubbish tip, but some allotments as well. If it wasn't burned there, I can't think where else it would have been burned. Strange thing to do, burn a body then move it. Why not leave it where it's been burned?'

'Puzzles us too.'

'Unpleasant job. It's that that got to me when I was in the fire service, getting up close and personal to a burned corpse...the smell...and to touch them...the flesh crumbles in your hand.'

'You had to touch them?'

'Oh...yes...the firefighters lift the corpses into the body bags and zip them up, not the ambulance crew or the mortuary van crews, but the poor old firefighters, and it really was that which reached me in the end... Been there, done that, got the T-shirt...there are other T-shirts to be had...and for doing equally useful jobs.'

'How do I find the place you speak of?'

'From here? With great difficulty. I'll show you.' She turned to Toby and said, 'Walk,' and the spaniel barked and turned in tight tail-wagging circles with excitement.

Having donned a duffle coat, woollen hat, scarf and gloves, Paula Eyton walked with Hennessey from her house back in the direction of the small wood in which the body was found, and then, after a hundred yards, she turned to her left down a narrow path between a house and garden on the left and a ploughed field on the right.

'I'd tuck your trousers into your socks if I were you...it can be muddy in parts here even when it's as cold as this.' She strode on, she safely in hiking boots, also recently donned.

Hennessey knelt and did as suggested and then followed her.

Paula Eyton turned on to a second path. 'This is why I couldn't direct you,' she said.

'Lots of paths hereabouts.'

Hennessey, having caught her up, grunted his appreciation, though he felt he could have easily followed her directions. Left out of the house, left on the path just before the field, left on to a second path; it was all that was needed.

The path led to a field which was as Paula Eyton had described, a hotchpotch of various land uses: waste tips, car dumps, a few tired looking allotments; an eyesore would, thought Hennessey, be an alternative description. 'If you'd allow me to continue alone?'

'Alone?' Paula Eyton inclined her head to one side. 'But I would have thought two people and a dog...'

'Alone,' Hennessey repeated. 'If you are correct and this is where the body was burned, then this is now a crime scene.'

'Ah, well, in that case...' She tugged the spaniel's lead. 'Come on, Toby, time to go home.' She walked away and then turned. 'Oh, sir...'

'Yes?' Hennessey also turned.

'The access road to this site is over there.' She pointed to the far end of the area of land as a gust of wind tugged the hair that protruded from the sides of her hat. 'It's the only way a vehicle can reach or leave the site.'

'Thank you.'

'And you could try Gladys.'

'Gladys?'

'Silver haired lady lives in the cottage.'

'The cottage?'

'The cottage...it's the only building on the road that runs to and from the site. She don't miss much, don't old Gladys,' she added in an affected accent. 'Not old Gladys.' She turned away and with her dark clothing, merged easily into the winter landscape.

Hennessey felt oddly alone. There were houses close by, the police were at the scene of the crime where the body lay under an inflatable tent, a mere fifteen minutes' walk away, yet he felt quite alone. The area had, he felt, a very lonely feel about it, very forlorn. Perhaps it was the abandoned cars, or the mounds of discarded refuse. Perhaps it was the solitary nature of the allotments which were scattered, rather than nestling cosily against each other, or it was the rooks and crows that fluttered and picked amongst the rubbish. Perhaps it may have been the denuded trees of the wood beyond the site, or the way the wind blew coldly and relentlessly from the east under a low, grey sky. Or perhaps it was because on this site a body had been burned. Whatever it was, Hennessey felt very alone in the world; he would be very pleased to quit this area.

He strolled over the ground, skirting round the abandoned cars and mounds of detritus, following rough paths that had been created over the passage of time and very soon found what he had been looking for. He found an area of flat concrete, about twenty feet by ten, the foundation for a building that had in the event not been constructed, like a pillbox for the Home Guard to use to defend Anslow against Hitler's tanks, or an air-raid shelter for the citizens of Anslow to use to shelter from Nazi bombs; it seemed to Hennessey to be of that vintage. It was still solid but had an aged and sun-bleached look. In the centre of the apron of concrete was a blackened area, oblong in shape, longer than it was wide but with an ill-defined edge, the sort of blackening he would have expected to be the result of a body being laid out and then set alight. He plunged his hand into his coat pocket and took out his mobile. He unfolded it and keyed in Yellich's number. He disliked mobile phones, or brain fryers as he referred to them, irritants in pubs and buses and destroyers of the romance of a train journey, but there was no denying their usefulness. 'Yellich?'

'Yes, boss?'

'I think I have found the place where the body was burned. Can you send SOCO here?'

'Yes, boss.'

'It's towards the village of Anslow. Just before they reach the village...well, at the beginning of the village really, there's a path going off to the right-hand side between a ploughed field and the side of someone's privet hedge, take a left on to another path and follow it to an area of desolation.'

'OK...right down a path at the entrance to the village, left on another path...an area of desolation?'

'That's it.'

'Sounds like an ideal place to burn a body,

skipper...has a very solemn feel.'

'Solemn is the word. There's something here that makes me shiver and it's not the wind.' He snapped his mobile shut and continued to prowl the area, looking at the ground from left to right and being careful to disturb as little as he could. Fifteen minutes later he noticed two men in high visibility jackets approach the wasteland. He raised his arm and walked towards them. 'Found me,' he said with a smile.

'Excellent directions, sir,' the older and taller of the two men replied warmly.

'Well, over here...' Hennessey led the two men to the concrete apron. 'Looks like a fire has been had here recently.'

'Smells like it too.' The older SOCO looked at the ground. 'I can smell it...very faint, but it's there...roast beef.'

Hennessey sniffed. 'Yes, you're right...this is the place. You know what to do...Photographs and then scrapings from the burned area...there will be human fat among the carbon.'

'He was deceased, sir.'

'You think?'

'The burned area is localized...well, he

certainly wasn't conscious, just as with the other two.'

'The other two?'

'Last Friday...I attended the other two burned corpses. I assume they are linked?'

'Just do your job,' Hennessey spoke calmly but with an air of authority, 'and I'll do mine.' He walked away and as he did so, he once again took out his mobile phone and phoned Yellich.

'What's happening, Yellich?'

'The body is being removed now...tent is being deflated.'

'Good...good...get the uniforms over here, this seems to be more of a crime scene than your location.'

'Yes, boss.'

'Do a fingertip search of this site. I am going to see Gladys.'

'Gladys?'

'So I believe is her name. She lives in the cottage, being the only building on the access road to this...this area of desolation.'

'The cottage...access road...got that boss ...so long as we know where you are.'

The cottage was easily found. As described by Paula Eyton, it was the only building on the access road to the area of desolation and to add to the distinctiveness it was, Hennessey saw, called 'The Cottage'. He walked up the concrete path and knocked on the door. There were two windows on the anterior of the cottage, one at either side of the door. The curtain to the left of the door moved as if in response to his knock. He stood on the threshold, looking about him at the trees to one side of the cottage, the ploughed field beyond, trees opposite. The nearest other dwellings were the roof-tops of the houses of Anslow. The door opened wide, Gladys revealed herself to be a frail looking woman with short cropped, grey hair. She had a steely look in her eyes and her jaw was set firm in what Hennessey thought could be best described as deter-mined.

'You really should have asked who I was before opening the door like that, Mrs...?'

'Gladys.' Her voice was cold, hard, but her mind was clearly all there, still firing on all cylinders. 'Just Gladys...and you are the police.'

'Yes.' He showed his ID.

'I don't need to see that, it's stamped on

your forehead. I saw you, was watching you with that woman from the village, her and her dog. I saw her lead you up to the allotments. She was happy with you behind her and then you stood next to her and said something and she went back towards the village, her and her dog, and you had a good poke about the allotments and then you talked into one of those things that people carry these days, then you came straight here and you were not bothered who saw you. You're a policeman alright. You better wipe your feet and come in.'

Hennessey scraped the mud from the soles of his shoes on a metal bar beside the door then, stooping, he entered the cottage. He found it cold inside, dark and cramped. He followed Gladys to a small parlour where two upright wooden chairs stood in front of an open fire grate. Combustibles and a lump of coal lay in the grate. Gladys sat in one of the chairs and pulled a red shawl round her shoulders. 'Better keep your coat on,' she said, pronouncing 'coat' as 'koy-it'. A Leeds accent, Hennessey thought. Definitely not York, not from Sheffield way either where coat is pronounced 'koo-at'. 'It's chilly.'

'You should light your fire, Gladys.'

'Not yet. Take a seat...you make me feel tired standing there.'

Hennessey sat down in the second upright chair. It creaked as he allowed his full weight to rest upon it.

'Not used to such weight, that old chair. Used to be my man's...it's nice to see a man sitting in it again. No, I keep a cold house, keeps me healthy. People got by without central heating for centuries...folks are just a lot of jessies now...I wear clothing to keep warm...I'll light the fire this after...I shouldn't burn coal but no one bothers old Gladys.'

'Very well, so long as you have heat if you need it.'

'I have. So you'll be wanting to know about the fire in the allotments last night?'

'Yes, yes, I would.'

'Used to be all allotments, forty, fifty years ago...all well tended...my man had one. Never tasted vegetables like the vegetables you grow in an allotment. Then one by one they got given up; no one wanted to take them over. Then a bit of rubbish was dumped, then another load, then the first motor was abandoned. There used to be thirty allotments on the plot, now there's five, and my husband's old allotment is home to an old car...aye...'

'The fire?' Hennessey pressed.

'What was burned, I don't know. Smelled...smelled wrong...went up quickly, in a flash. They used petrol I should think. Whatever, it went up with a whoosh. They stepped back smartly.'

'They?'

'A man and a woman. Did they burn it on the concrete?'

'Yes.'

'That was laid some years ago, it was going to be a storeroom for the allotment tenants but they couldn't get planning permission.'

'Oh, was that it? I thought perhaps...'

'Laid the foundations and then thought they ought to get permission to build the thing.' Gladys's chest heaved as she laughed. 'Silly sausages. Anyway, the concrete stayed...it looked to be about where the fire was.'

'Yes, it was.'

'About the only place you could have a

bonfire.' Which, thought Hennessey, is more accurate than you know, having once read that 'bonfire' is a contraction of 'bone fire', being the final disposal of the remains of a felon who had been hung, drawn and quartered. A bonfire was exactly what this lady had witnessed.

'Saw it from the window upstairs...at the back.'

'What time was that?'

'About eleven p.m. Not after midnight, I go to my bed at midnight as the bells chime ...and I don't get up until dawn, not for nobody. Just Gladys in her old cocoon, snug and warm. So it was before midnight but late...heard the van first.'

'The van?'

'Like a small car, but a van...I know the difference.'

'Yes.'

'I heard it turn into the lane. Never seen it before but the driver seemed to know where he was. I thought another car was being dumped...watched it go. White...it was white...no writing on the side...sure of that ...so then I went upstairs and saw nothing, it was all hidden from view, then whoosh...a

193

flash of flame and in the light of the flame I saw two figures. I thought...I thought male and female, then the flames died down after a few minutes, then it was like they were put out. The figures started to smother the flames...then it was dark...then, some time later, after the van drove back down the lane, didn't see it but heard it. Gladys was well abed by then.'

It was Wednesday, 13.20 hours.

George Hennessey walked across the car park of York District Hospital, digesting a hurried but satisfying lunch. He glanced to his right as he walked towards the slab-sided, medium rise building. His heart warmed as he saw it, that beautiful old lady, a red and white Riley RMA circa 1947, the only car of its type in the city, nay in the Vale of York. One lady owner, lovingly serviced by a garage whose proprietor had made the owner promise him first refusal should she ever decide to sell the vehicle. It was an offer said lady owner was pleased to give, if only to ensure high quality maintenance, knowing that she would never sell the vehicle: it had belonged to her father and she, in the fullness of time, was going to bequeath it to her son. It was not, Hennessey pondered, as he turned once more towards the building, every heirloom that does 10,000 trouble-free miles from year end to year end, requiring little more than an annual service and a change of tyres.

He pushed open the door of the hospital building and was met by a blast of warm air which caused him to instantly remove his hat, scarf and gloves, and to fully open his coat front. He walked down the softly echoing corridor, undertaking a walk he had taken many times before but did so with a lightness of step despite the heavy task ahead. He walked to the Department of Pathology and after presenting at the reception desk, walked down a smaller corridor and tapped softly on a door.

'Come in.'

Hennessey entered the room. It was a small, cramped office.

'Knew it was you.' Dr D'Acre glanced up at him. 'It wasn't just that I was expecting you but more that I would know that knock anywhere. The classic copper's knock, tap, tap...tap. Do take a seat.'

Hennessey sat beside her desk, noting a photograph of three children and a second photograph showing a horse which, even to Hennessey's untrained eye, looked to be a magnificent animal. 'I must alter my style.' He lowered himself on to the chair, holding his hat, gloves and scarf on his lap.

'So...' Dr D'Acre leaned back avoiding eye contact with him. 'Number three?'

'Possibly...it is going to throw a spanner in the works if he or she...'

'He.'

'I see...well, if he is not connected in any way with Mr and Mrs Dent.'

'You're thinking a serial killer?'

'Yes. If he is not connected, then yes, I am afraid that's what we are looking at. Just when we had someone in the frame...at least getting into the frame...just needed a push.'

'Oh?'

'Yes...the first two victims were husband and wife.'

'I know.'

'Yes...sorry. They adopted two children... one, the boy, Gregory, is a chilling piece of work. Set to inherit millions upon his adoptive parents' death...amoral...His adoptive parents' cats disappeared, their dog died shortly after he arrived and shortly after it had growled at him.'

Dr D'Acre raised her eyebrows and allowed herself uncharacteristic eye contact with him. 'I wouldn't dismiss that. I mean an animal's reaction to someone.'

'Oh, I don't...we don't. Can't use it as evidence of course, but it points us in the right direction. People reporting paranormal experiences have done the same...but it was a very brittle alibi.'

'Oh?'

'Yes, his lady friend said she was with him.'

'I see.'

'But there was no other independent witness. She's as cold and hardhearted as he is and they are an item. She stands to gain much from his bereavement, even if he pays her for her alibi and then they go their own separate ways. That is a very brittle alibi.' He glanced around the cramped office, neatly kept desk, calendar on the wall. 'So that was the state of play until, as you suggest, number three turned up. It was going to be a question of putting pressure on the alibi, see if it would break. We advised his lady friend, Susan Thurnham, the ice maiden, of the consequences of aiding and abetting, especially in a crime as serious as murder – double murder, in fact. She just smiled and said "Really?" or "Is that so?" or some such non-chalance. But now with number three on the slab...no wonder he is cocky and she self-assured. If there's no connection between the victims, we are looking at a serial killer.'

'Well, I wish you luck. I can tell you that the victim is a male, probably late middle age or even elderly, he was not burned where he was found...'

'Yes, we believe we have identified the location where the body was burned. It poses another mystery.'

'Oh?'

'Well...the location of the burning seems to have been an area once given over to thriving and productive allotments, now given over to the unlawful disposal of waste, old cars and other refuse...and which is reasonably well hidden from the road. And further, which is less than a quarter of a mile from where the body was found.'

'So, why move the body at all? Is that what you mean?'

'Yes. A curiosity more than a mystery, but it's intriguing.'

'Well, I would say there's either a good reason to move the body or no logical reason at all. It might be just a panic re- action kicking in. Dare say all will be revealed. Well, I took a rectal temperature, despite the evident thermal confusion, which indicated recent death, within hours of him being found, but I don't like to be drawn on the time of death as you know. So all I will say, is that it was within hours of the corpse being discovered, and anything else I can tell you will have to wait until after the post-mortem. Well, Mr Filey will have prepped the body by now. Shall we get changed? I'll see you in the theatre.'

'Good old dog walkers.' Hennessey stood.

'What?' Dr D'Acre shot a glance at him.

'Oh, nothing...nothing...just an old man mumbling to himself.'

'Not so old.' She allowed herself a rare smile. 'I'll see you in there.'

It was Wednesday, December 17, 14.30 hours.

Six

Wednesday, December 17, 23.10 hours
*in which Somerled Yellich meets a mystic
and the gracious reader is privy to George
Hennessey's ghosts.*

Sometimes, Somerled Yellich had found, sometimes, you just know who you are talking to. This, he felt, was one such case.

'It's now twenty-four hours.' The woman was elderly, tearful, agitated. 'I just know something bad has happened to him.'

'When did you last see your husband, Mrs Harthill?'

'Yesterday morning. He went out...for his walk...he's got high blood pressure and the doctors told him to take exercise as a way of controlling it. Don't have to go to a gym, he said. I mean, a gym at Arthur's age, but it's not necessary he said, a good, brisk twenty-minute walk each day, that ought to do the trick, and Arthur...he always went the second mile, you know...so he went out for a forty-minute walk each morning, only really bad weather would keep him in.'

'Don't talk as though he is no longer with us.' Yellich spoke in as reassuring a manner as he could muster, but he had to concede that Mrs Harthill's concern was probably with some foundation and his 'inner voice' as he often called it, or 'his waters', knew that Mr Arthur Harthill was at that moment a charred corpse in the pathology laboratory at York District Hospital, probably then being or indeed having been, dissected to establish the cause of his death, if it was, by some means, not the fire.

'He walks out by the wood, you see...'

'The wood?'

'Penny Wood.'

'OK.'

'But he never returned. Always the same walk. He takes it when the weather's fine, so I know the route and I went looking for him, calling his name...Arthur...Arthur...I called ...no reply, and the wood is clear this time of the year.'

'Clear?'

'No leaves.'

'Ah...'

'You can see all around you, but it's like the earth swallowed him up or he's been abducted by them aliens like you hear about on television. Vanished. We grew up together ...same street...we used to play together when we were four or five years old, now we are both seventy. We've known each other for sixty-five years, married for fifty of them. We always said when the first one went, the other wouldn't be too far behind.'

'Mrs Harthill...'

'He's gone...I know he's gone.' She opened her handbag and took out a photograph and handed it to Yellich. 'It's the most recent.'

Yellich took the photograph and looked at it. He saw Mrs Harthill glance from side to side as if seizing the opportunity to look at the interview room, spartan and functional as it was: a desk, three upright chairs, hessian carpeting, two-tone orange walls, light above dark. The photograph showed a slender, cheery-looking man digging a garden.

'Side on,' Yellich commented.

'Yes...it's a game we play, taking photographs of each when the other isn't looking; we've got some grand snaps like that over the years. Isn't it any use?'

'Oh...it's of use. May we keep it?'

'Yes, that's what I brought it for, for you to keep.'

'Thanks.' Yellich clipped the photograph to the file he had opened on Harthill, Arthur, missing person. 'Do you have a photograph of Mr Harthill showing his face?'

'Like a passport photograph?'

'Yes...but a bit larger.'

'Yes.' She nodded. She was a small, frail looking woman, finely made, with short, close cropped silver hair, but she seemed to Yellich to have a strong character, a woman, he thought, who could weather a severe storm and possibly she had indeed done so, but he also felt that she was quite correct when she said that she and her husband would die within a short space of time...in her seventies...together since childhood, one would pine without the other. 'Yes, I can let you have quite a lot like that, photography is our passion.'

'Just one good one will do.' Yellich paused and then asked, 'What did your husband do for a living?'

Mrs Harthill hesitated before answering and then said, 'So, he is dead? I am right; he's a corpse somewhere, isn't he?'

Yellich made to speak but remained silent.

'You wouldn't have asked that question if he was just a missing person...not at his age. You've got a body of a man that you can't... that you don't know who it is...his identity. That's the word, his identity...you don't know his identity.'

'Possibly.' Yellich looked at the surface of the table. 'We possibly have...a male was taken to the mortuary of the York District Hospital earlier today.'

'Oh...my. Well, he was a surface worker.'

'A surface worker?'

'At the colliery...Wistow Pit. He wouldn't ever go into the cages and go underground but he worked on the surface. Less money but he wasn't bothered. He was safe on the surface. He always said that mining is a safe job, though you hear about accidents because often a large number of men are lost, but if you want a dangerous job, go and work on a farm, that's what Arthur would say. He said, on average, one person a week is killed on British farms...one agricultural worker. Fifty miners a year are not killed... and we got our monthly ton.'

'Monthly ton?'

'Each worker and retired worker at the pit gets a ton of coal a month, left in our drive-way, and Arthur or me would put it in the coalhole, shovel it in, one shovel full at a time...was a half-day job. Really, we could have left it where it was because no one would steal it. Coal Board houses, you see. Everybody worked in the pit, every home had a ton of coal put in their drive each month, but we had to move it because it was an eyesore. It was a condition of receiving it...it had to be put in the coalhole out of sight and the drive swept up. What happened?'

'To the man? I can't tell you. I won't tell you until...unless it is your husband, then I will, but we may be jumping the gun...but...'

'But.' She fixed him with a keen, piercing stare. 'But what?'

'Well, I would like to drive you home, see

where you and Mr Harthill live.'

'Lived,' she said. 'We used to live there. I still do...but not for long, I think. Not for long.' She stood. 'I am feeling tired, anyway...won't complain when my time comes. Come on.'

Yellich had never been to the Throwley estate before. He found it a strange, but not uninteresting experience. The houses he saw were drab, uniformly so, grey with small and often unkempt gardens. What Yellich did find fascinating was the smell of burning coal which lingered in the air of the estate, smelling it even before he halted his car. When he did halt the car outside Mrs Harthill's house and left the vehicle, walking with her up her drive to the rear of the house, he, for the first time in his life smelled air that was heavy with coal smoke. He understood how it could be harmful to health and clearly understood then the need for smokeless zones, but he had to concede that the smell had warmth about it. He thought the smell welcoming and homely. In the neighbouring drive was a pile of coal, just as Mrs Harthill had described.

'They're away,' Mrs Harthill explained, as

if apologizing for her neighbours. 'They'll put it away when they get back. Their daughter lives in Cornwall, she's having her first baby, they're going down for the event. They went down as parents and hope to come back as grandparents.'

'Ah...'

'You have children?'

'One...a boy.'

'Plan any more?' She fished into her coat pocket and withdrew a large mortice key which she placed into the lock of the door.

'No,' Yellich replied softly, 'no. Myself and Mrs Yellich are content with the one.'

'He'll need a brother or a sister.' She pushed open the door, forcing it with her shoulder. 'Arthur was going to fix this door...it jams.'

'He's got special needs.' Yellich assisted her to open the door. 'So...one it is. We couldn't manage with two.'

'Special needs? You mean he's simple?'

'Well, that's not the term...'

'Sorry...there's a girl like that on the estate ...she always seems such a happy soul...bless her.'

The house was neatly kept. Mrs Harthill

had made up a fire before she left the house, safely behind a fireguard. It had settled by the time she and Yellich returned, into a bed of hot coal and gave out what Yellich found to be a very solid form of heat. Mrs Harthill peeled off her coat. 'Can't beat a coal fire,' she said. 'My sister and her husband live in York on the Tang Hall estate...you'll know it.'

'Oh, yes.'

'Aye...they got a lot of bother on that estate.'

'Yes.'

'Her house has central heating and gas fires...it's not the same.'

'I can tell.'

'Not used to coal fires? You'll be too young to remember them.'

'Yes, we were like your sister, gas fires and central heating.'

'Well, give me coal...despite the mess you have to clear up each day. So, what can I do? What can I do to help you catch Arthur's killer?'

'Mrs Harthill, we still don't know it is your husband.'

'It's him.' She touched her chest, 'I know...

in here I know. I told you, Arthur and I knew each other since we were pre-school age and yesterday, about midday, I felt a sensation...not a physical thing...up here.' She pointed to her head. 'Up here I felt...a feeling that I couldn't recognize...I have never felt it before in my life and so I didn't know what it was, but it's stayed, it hasn't gone away and this morning I knew what it was...it was loneliness. No wonder I didn't recognize it...loneliness. I've heard folk talk about it, I've read of things called lonely hearts' clubs, never knew what they were but now I do...it's Arthur. For the first time in fifty years I woke up alone, alone in my bed, alone in my house. He was killed about midday yesterday...in the middle of his walk. Not natural causes, either. I was alone very suddenly. I felt as if I had been robbed of something. I wouldn't have felt like that if he had had a heart attack...that would have been sudden...possibly...but this was sudden, sudden...just before the midday news came on television. Sudden...but it was not fair, like I had been robbed...like something had been stolen from me. If Arthur had had a heart attack, I wouldn't have felt that I had been robbed. I would still have missed him but it would have been different.'

'I see.' Yellich held eye contact with Mrs Harthill, once again being impressed by her strength of character and sharp mind.

'We were spiritualists,' she explained. 'We were both that way inclined for a long time. We just feel things that other folk don't seem to feel. I just know that he was killed at noon yesterday.' She paused. 'You know, I think I could take you to the very place he was killed.'

'Oh...?'

'Yes. We used to walk at the same speed, we could follow his route. He left here at 11.30 a.m. yesterday morning, so we walk for half an hour, that's all we have to do... and I know where that will take us. Half an hour's walk from here will take us to the one place on his route which can't be seen... what's that word?'

'Overlooked?'

'Yes...overlooked. It's not long, about twice the distance from here to the bottom of the garden.' She pointed to the window.

Yellich glanced out of the window at a flat expanse of lawn which terminated at a wooden fence, beyond which was the garden belonging to another house on the estate, from the chimney of which smoke rose to be caught and whisked away by the wind. About thirty feet, he thought, that would be twice the length of Mrs Harthill's back garden. More than enough space to murder someone, drag their body deeper into the wood. 'Yes, alright, we'll do that... but first...'

'A photograph...full face.'

'Yes, please, and, if you have one, a strand of his hair.'

'A strand of his hair?'

'Yes, if you could find one...perhaps from the bath plughole, or from his comb. We could confirm...I mean, if he is the gentleman that was admitted...whose corpse was brought to the hospital this morning.'

'You could tell if it's Arthur...just by a strand of hair?'

'Yes...well, we can't, our scientists can... out at Wetherby...that's where they are based, but yes, it will confirm identity, probably more than the photograph.'

'I'll get his comb.'

★ ★ ★

'Here,' Mrs Harthill stopped. 'Here...this is where Arthur would have been at midday yesterday. I can't say that I feel anything... but I never have been sensitive to location. Arthur was...you know we'd be walking and he'd stop and say something happened here ...something violent...he'd be sensitive like that. I never was...but I see ghosts that other folk don't see...that is my curse.'

'Curse?'

'I thought it was a gift when I realized I was seeing ghosts, but it has become a curse ...I feel no sense of presence here... though this is where Arthur would have been at about midday yesterday.'

Yellich glanced at the path ahead of him. It was indeed a perfect place for an ambush. The path was sunken and curved; it was not overlooked by any building nor any roadway or pavement. The wood was generously covered in shrubs, few, very few with leaves, but sufficient shrubbery to conceal a body from the view of any person walking the pathway if it was dragged far enough and then perhaps covered with something, a sheet of corrugated iron, an old carpet, left as if selfishly fly-tipped. The path emerged on to a road, Yellich could hear the cars. Overpower an elderly man, conceal his body, return at night, carry the body the short distance to a waiting vehicle and drive it away to where it was burned. 'We'd better walk back the way we came.'

'Why? It's quicker to carry on, brings you back to the estate. Arthur was just ten minutes from home.'

'Yes.' Yellich turned to her. 'I can smell the coal fire smoke from here, but this is a crime scene. I'd rather not contaminate it any more than it has already been contaminated. So, if you don't mind...?'

A lone crow cawed.

Hennessey sat back in his chair, cradling the mug of tea, listening to what Somerled Yellich said.

'So,' he said as he glanced out of the window at the ribbon of street lamps on Micklegate and the last remnants of daylight in a dark sky, 'too late to do a fingertip search today, as you say...but tomorrow?'

'First thing, skipper. I don't think the crime scene will get contaminated overnight ...no one will visit it. I mean, if the felon or

214

felons dropped something incriminating and it hasn't been picked up yet, it will still be there in the morning.'

'Yes...well, can you get the comb off to Wetherby by courier? Dr D'Acre sent tissue samples to them with a case reference number. Ask them to match them to the DNA from the comb, if you would and if they can. Listening to what you have said, I tend to think they will, though that does rather throw a spanner into the works.'

'You think a serial killer, sir?'

'Yes.' Hennessey placed the mug on his desk. 'Yes, I am beginning to think that way. No link between Mr Harthill and the Dents?'

'None that we could find. Mrs Harthill doesn't know them and they are a different social class. The Dents were senior professionals living...well, you remember their house...West End House in the east end of the village of Great Sheldwich.'

'Yes.'

'Well, the Harthill household was the opposite end of the social ladder...almost. A Coal Board owned house, when there was a Coal Board, owned by a mining company

215

now. Still burning coal; never came across a lot of coal fires before, it was interesting – the smell in the street, the solid feeling of the warmth.'

'Yes, it would have taken me back to Greenwich, we burned coal in our fire...all Londoners did...terrible smogs though. When the smoke from the thousands of coal fires mingles with fog, whenever there was a fog, it was called a smog, cobbling together the words smoke and fog.'

'I see.'

'Caused many fatalities. People who had chest problems at the best of times succumbed, forced the passing of the Clean Air Acts and the introduction of smokeless fuel, but nothing beats coal for warmth, provided you can get rid of the smoke. I would like to have smelled coal fire smoke once more. Pockets of coal-burning houses still exist, Grassington for one, but I didn't know about the Throwley estate...out by Wistow, you say?'

'Yes, boss.'

'Might take a trip out there one day, a lesson in modern history for myself. Well, back to business, the post-mortem on the third victim...apparent third victim provided the same result as the PMs on Mr and Mrs Dent.'

'Dead before being burned?' Yellich drained his mug of tea and placed it on Hennessey's desk.

'Yes, fortunately for him, no soot in the trachea, death was caused by a massive blow to the head, he was struck from behind. The pathway seems a likely murder place you think?'

'Yes, it runs the risk of someone coming along unexpectedly but that section of the path cannot be overlooked, it would be a good place to do it. Drag the body into the shrubs, out of sight from the path, return after dark to collect the corpse and remove it to where it was burned.'

'Local knowledge.'

'Sorry, boss?'

'Local knowledge...that wood.'

'Penny Wood.'

'Yes, the stretch of sunken pathway, the desolate allotment site, the move to the other wood where it was found, that all says local knowledge, as does the location where the Dents were found...by the river, I mean.

No one...no one in their right mind would go near a river, or any stretch of water at night, it's far too dangerous unless they knew exactly where they were, unless they knew every square foot of ground and I can't see Gregory Dent having that level of knowledge – he's too much of a playboy type.'

'Seems so...seems we were barking up the wrong tree with respect of Mr Dent. Wrong part of the forest completely, as you said.'

'So what now, boss?'

'Well, if you'll organize the fingertip search tomorrow and have the comb sent to Wetherby, I'll go and see the Commander ...We need an "ologist".'

Yellich smiled. 'Yes, boss.' He stood and left Hennessey's office.

Hennessey, somewhat wearily, walked to the office of Commander Sharkey. He tapped reverently on the door.

'Come.' The voice had an imperious tone and the answer came only after a noticeable pause.

Hennessey opened the door and approached Sharkey's desk. 'A word, please, sir.'

'Of course, George, take a pew.'

Hennessey sat in one of the chairs in front of Sharkey's desk. Once again the desktop was neat, not a thing out of place. Sharkey, younger than Hennessey, was as usual, impeccably dressed; behind him were framed photographs, one of a younger Sharkey as a junior officer in the British Army and a second of Sharkey in the uniform of the Royal Hong Kong Police.

'So –' Sharkey sat back in his chair – 'what can I do for you, George?'

'Well, to cut to the chase, sir, I think we need help. As I said to Sergeant Yellich just now, we need an "ologist".'

'A psychologist?'

'I believe that is the...title, yes, sir.'

'A forensic psychologist?'

'Well, someone who can tell us how a criminal mind works...how a felon ticks.'

'A forensic psychologist.'

'You have to approve the funding, sir.'

'Yes...so why do we need the services of the "ologist"?'

Hennessey told him.

'I see.' Sharkey leaned forward when Hennessey had finished talking. 'So, three murders...all similar, no connection between the first two and the third, but the first two were husband and wife?'

'It seems to be the beginning of a pattern. I'd like to stop it before it gets worse.'

'Yes...yes, I can sympathize...and serial murderers have been known to target members of the same family. So yes, I'll set the wheels in motion. Do you have anyone in mind?'

'We've used Dr Joseph at the university before, sir. She was very helpful the last time.'

'Alright, leave that with me.' Sharkey wrote on his pad. 'What is her first name?'

'Kamy...short for Kamilla, spelled with a *k*.'

'Alright...now, George, since you are here, how are you finding things?'

'I am not ready to police a desk, sir. I am on top of things. You have told me about your maths teacher at your school, Johnny Hay.'

'Taighe.' Sharkey nodded. 'Taighe, Johnny Taighe. Yes, just when he should have been allowed to soft-pedal into his pension they piled on the pressure. Poor bloke deserved

retirement...he'd earned it teaching practi-
cally all his working life but always lower
school, then they make him teach senior
school for national qualifications.'

'Couldn't handle it.'

'No...I think about him often as I get
older. He made more of an impact, more of
an impression than I thought at the time.'

'Yes, that happens.'

'Poor old boy...equipped to carry the sort
of load you put on a milk float and they give
him the sort of load you would put on the
back of an articulated lorry.'

'Well, I am well up to the job still, sir. I
hear my pension calling my name but I am
not ready to go yet.'

'Good...well I won't let what happened to
Johnny Taighe happen to any one of mine.
So, if you feel that you are losing the edge, if
it should come to feel too much, you know
where I am; we'll work something out.'

'I appreciate it, sir, but I walked out of the
Navy after National Service by walking off a
destroyer in Portsmouth Harbour, not from
behind a desk, and I'd like to walk into
retirement from the coalface of police work.
My career has always been one of criminal

investigation...I'd like my last day in the job to be just that.'

'Very well.' Sharkey held up his hand. 'Just so long as you know that you can knock on my door. So what about the nick as a whole, anything I should worry about? I had my fill of corruption in there. He pointed to the photograph of himself when in the Royal Hong Kong Police. 'I wasn't in that organization very long, thank goodness, but I was there and part of it. If you were in it, you were part of it.'

This time Hennessey held up his hand. 'Sir, with respect, I am certain there is no corruption here. I would have sensed it, I am sure. I really think that you can sleep at night on that score.'

'Well, thank you, George. I find that re-assuring. So, I'll acquire funding for Dr Joseph's services, let you know when you can make contact with her.'

Hennessey stood. 'Thank you, sir.'

Hennessey returned to his office, collected his hat and coat and drove home to Easing-wold. He disliked driving for one tragic and highly personal reason, and the slow, halting rush-hour drive on that dark evening he found less than pleasant, but his heart leapt as he approached his house because there, half on and half off the kerb stood a BMW in German racing silver. Whoever was awaiting him at home would more than compensate for the irritating drive.

Later, after handshakes and the How are you's, George and Charles Hennessey sat in the kitchen of George Hennessey's house, the same house in which Charles had grown up.

'Copycat?' Charles sipped his tea and reached for a toasted teacake.

'Probably...if it's not a serial killer, it has to be a copycat. I don't know which is worse. A serial killer won't stop until he is caught or he "matures", so I once read, but it means just one felon to catch. A copycat will probably stop at one but it means an entirely separate additional investigation. Ah well, keeps us busy.'

'No shortage of work for you to do,' Charles said with a smile. 'And keep us busy.'

'What are you doing at the moment? Still in Sheffield?'

'No...no...that trial finished. We won an acquittal.'

'Good for you.'

'Well...yes, chalk it up but it wasn't a pleasing case. We knew he did it, but it was our job to make the Crown work to prove their case and we managed to do that. The jury must have agonized but in the end there just was insufficient evidence to make his prosecution safe. The Crown's case was like a colander...had too many holes. It was as though they had hoped for a lazy defence team because they knew he was guilty.'

'Instead they got you. You always were a fighter.'

'Well, me and my junior; he's going far at the bar, he's like a pit bull terrier. He cross-examined the police witness. He's still very junior but his technique is awesome, you could almost see the senior police officer backing up against his attack. You'd think he was a QC with decades of experience. I am learning from him, but I think he should develop a more sophisticated approach. I enjoy tripping witnesses up with a calm and deceptively gentle approach, it lowers their guard. My junior's approach ensures that their guard is always well up, but it's not often that a senior police officer looks

cowed in the dock...Anyway, the felon walked. In Scotland it would have been a "not
proven" verdict. Very useful third verdict
they have up there, but here and in Wales it
is only guilty or not guilty. Couldn't convict
on the evidence presented...too fragile...so
they had to acquit, but that didn't mean to
say he was innocent and his sneer when the
foreperson said "not guilty" said so.'

'It happens. He walks only to be nailed for
something else at some future date.'

'Oh, indeed. No...this week I'm in Bradford and this time we are also going not
guilty, but this time I really do believe our
client to have been wrongly charged, so we
are fighting for the right reason. We're giving
it everything we've got. I would be very
upset if this man is convicted.'

'The case against him must be strong.'

'It is...motive, witnesses...He has no alibi,
he also has a previous criminal record for
acts of violence, so he's no saint, but that
doesn't mean he's guilty of this offence.
Anyway, we'll do what we can and lodge an
appeal if the jury find against him.'

'Anyway, how are the children?'

'Fine...thriving, barrelling through their

milestones, wanting to see Grandad again.'

'And Grandad wants to see them again. Soon.'

'This weekend?' Charles Hennessey raised an eyebrow.

'Mmm...possibly.'

'Ah ha...your lady friend, whom we still haven't met.'

'Well, it is my weekend off, one weekend in five when I don't have to work Saturday or Sunday. We had planned something, but this case...burning elderly people...no leads ...dead-end alleys every way we look.'

'Well, you should take time off, you deserve it. It's only now I have children that I realize how hard it was for you, bringing me up alone.'

'I had help.'

'Childminders...not the same as a partner. So you deserve a rest, enjoy your weekend.'

'I will, if I can, but my friend will understand. I confess my retirement looms not like an end but a beginning. I will have so much time to do all the things I want to do and a good pension to enable me to do them. I intend to start each morning with a warm bath; no more falling out of bed and pulling on my clothes as if on automatic pilot, and driving to work whilst still half asleep. Not a lot of driving either, that is going to be the best part. Everything I need is in walking distance. I'll take the bus and the train if I need to go anywhere.'

'Uncle Graham's death really did affect you, didn't it?'

'Yes...me and Graham...' George Hennessey bit his lip. 'Yes...as you know, there were eight years between us, so we never had that sibling rivalry that occurs when children are born within a year or two of each other. Him and his beloved motorbike...used to help him clean it on Sunday mornings, then he'd take me up to town, see the sights: Trafalgar Square, the Palace, the Houses of Parliament, across Westminster Bridge and back to Greenwich. Then one day, when I was...well, a lad, he rode away one night and I never saw him again. Your grandparents identified the body but the last I saw was a coffin being lowered into the ground on a summer's day...Same as your mother's funeral, except of course she wasn't buried – she's out there in the garden so she could watch you growing up. But yes, there is a gap and yes...yes, it has left me with an abiding dislike of the internal combustion engine whether two wheels or four...whether two stroke or four...a life for a patch of oil.'

'We've never really spoken about it before. Is that what caused the accident?'

'So we were told, though accident investigation is much more sophisticated now, but at the time we were told he hit a patch of oil on the road, lost control...a few inches either way, he might have missed it. You'd have liked him, he had a very warm personality and was wasted in the bank... but he was getting out, much to the dismay of our parents who thought the bank was "safe", which it was. It wasn't Graham, he was too creative to be a banker. He had applied for art college, he wanted to be a photojournalist...he would have been good at that...he would have taken some impressive, heart-stopping photographs...but...'

'But...'

When Charles Hennessey had warmly taken his leave, George Hennessey settled down to his evening. After briefly telling Jennifer of his day, briefly because the east wind was biting, he prepared a simple but wholesome meal and digested it whilst sitting in front of a fire of faggots he had collected and allowed to dry. He sat down to read a book that had been in his collection of military history for many years but which he had only by then found time to read. It was an intriguing account of the Gallipoli campaign of 1915 told from the Turkish perspective. It had been translated into English in 1935 and was, Hennessey thought, written with an economical and very readable style and lavishly illustrated with maps and ink drawings. He thought it a gem of a book and an utter steal for the few pence he'd paid for it from a stall in the open market in York one summer's day. He had squandered money on occasions but over the years he had found that squandering was compensated by bargains acquired and money well spent. That book was one such bargain, and an example of how great joy and satisfaction can be had in exchange for a modest outlay.

Later, his meal settled, and Oscar fed, they walked together, man and dog, half an hour out, fifteen minutes allowing the mongrel to explore a small copse and half an hour back.

Later still, George Hennessey, collar up-turned, scarf around his neck and hat screwed on tight, walked into Easingwold for a pint of brown and mild at the Dove Inn. Just one before last orders were called. On the return journey he remembered to check a report he had read that one of the seven stars of the Great Bear had begun to flicker as its first stage of dying. He saw that it was so, that the most famous of the constellations was soon, though probably not even in his grandchildrens' lifetime, going to be six stars.

'There has to be another one.'

'Another!'

'Yes...soon...tonight. The plan is working ...don't you see it's working. There is no other way.' The man paused. The woman beside him smiled. 'Don't you see, there is no other way...we have to see this through.'

The fourth person in the room put his hand to his head and groaned.

'Doesn't matter how many you kill,' said the first man, 'you still only serve one life sentence...and if we keep our heads, if we stick to the plan, we won't serve any sentence at all. Just one more, that will do it. Just one more.'

Wilson Weston walked home along Bad Bargain Lane towards Tang Hall. He thrust his hands deep in his pockets, the wind tugged at his wispy, grey hair, and sliced through his clothing and chilled his bald head. He wished he had brought his cap. He walked on; he would soon be home, very soon be home. He wasn't a young man, if he was young he would have run, run to keep warm, run to get out of the wind, but not anymore, those days were gone...but the lights of the Tang Hall estate were ahead of him. The van drove past slowly and halted a little way ahead. The man thought it suspicious. It was a van, a two-seater; he might be being offered a lift by a good soul were it not for the fact that as the van passed he saw, very clearly, that the passenger seat was occupied. There was no other reason for any vehicle to stop on Bad Bargain Lane, there were no buildings, just fields at either side. Wilson Weston halted. He was suspicious. The van had seemed to halt for some reason in relation to him. There was nothing coincidental about the vehicle stopping, no other foot passengers, or any other vehicles on that dark, starlit night to make the van draw to a halt just ahead of him. The van lay between Wilson Weston and home, just sitting there, white exhaust fumes rising briefly from the tail pipe before being snatched away by the wind. He stood there. The van remained motionless. Then the white reversing lights came on, the van whined towards him in reverse gear and Wilson Weston intuitively knew that there was nothing to be gained by running.

Seven

Thursday, December 18,
10.15 hours – 22.47 hours
*in which a breakthrough is made and the
kind reader is privy to the joy in the life of
Somerled Yellich and also the joy in the life
of George Hennessey.*

George Hennessey stepped out of the white
inflatable tent and looked around him. Sergeant Yellich looked at him, waiting for a
lead, a response, as did a number of constables and a sergeant, but all Hennessey could
do was absorb the scene – woodland – and
note the weather: low, grey sky, cold easterly
wind. He approached Yellich. 'Woodland
again.'

'Yes, sir.'

'Four...'

'Yes, sir...in almost as many days.'

'And again it was a dog walker who found the body.'

'Yes, sir, understandable though...I mean, this time of year, mid-week, the only folk who go into woodland are dog walkers.'

'Dare say.' He turned and noticed a line of houses in the middle distance. 'Better do a house-to-house along that street, somebody might have seen something.'

'I'll get on it, boss.'

'Good. Who is this guy...?'

'Persons, sir.' Yellich smiled.

'Sorry?'

'Persons...we have already concluded that this is the work of at least two persons.'

'Yes...sorry...so, who are these people?'

Yellich shrugged. 'I'll organize a fingertip search of the area...then start the house-to-house. Dr D'Acre is expected.'

'Yes, thank you...thank you.' He replied in an absentminded, detached attitude. Again he asked himself, Who are these people? Movement to his right caught his eye, he turned and saw the slender figure of Dr D'Acre, followed by a constable who carried her Gladstone bag. She was solemn-faced with what Hennessey saw to be a determined look about her. She allowed herself brief eye contact with Hennessey as she closed his personal space. 'Good morning, ma'am.' Hennessey touched the brim of his hat.

'Chief Inspector.' She wore short hair, no make-up and carried herself erect; there was not even the slightest leaning forwards or hunching of shoulders as, Hennessey had often noticed, with many tall women. She wore green coveralls, solid, sensible shoes, and a woollen hat. Unusual for her, noted Hennessey, rarely having seen her in a hat, but he could understand the need for it; the wind was a biter. She glanced at the tent. 'Another burned corpse, I understand?' She took her bag from the constable with a nod of thanks.

'Yes, Doctor.' Hennessey walked back to the inflatable tent and held the flap aside. Dr D'Acre stooped and entered the tent. Hennessey followed. The corpse was lying on its side and had, when contracting in the flames, adopted the classic pugilistic pose.

'Male.' Dr D'Acre knelt and placed her bag on the ground. 'Placed here but not burned here: the grass is not fire damaged and it's unusual for a burns victim to be on their side, though this is probably not a burns victim. If the pattern is establishing itself, this gentleman was deceased when he was set alight, so his body was burned after death, we hope. Again, the burning is not as extensive as it might otherwise have been... again, there is a sense that the fire was not allowed to run its course. Either it was put out, or died out because of lack of oxygen.' She opened her bag and removed a rectal thermometer. 'This might give some indication of the time of death but...well...we have had this conversation before.'

'Yes, indeed.' Hennessey smiled. 'The cause, yes, but the when...no...just a very wide approximation.'

'Well, when he was last seen alive, and when his body was found, is as good an approximation as anything I can offer, as I have said many, many times before, but a rectal temperature and a ground temperature is part of the procedure...so...'

'Understood and appreciated.'

'I understand...' Dr D'Acre said as she inserted the thermometer into the rectum of the corpse, 'I understand that the third victim...'

'Mr Harthill?'

'Was that his name? Well, the third victim was burned out of doors.'

'Yes.'

'Well, he too was not burned as badly as otherwise might have been the case so, if he was burned outside, there was no shortage of oxygen.'

'No...no, there wouldn't be, would there?'

'Well, that means that the fire was extinguished, it didn't die from oxygen starvation.'

'So it was put out?'

'Yes...smothered by blankets or similar... or doused with water. For some reason, the fire was not allowed to run its course.'

'What possible reason?'

'Ah...that, Chief Inspector, is your territory.' She extracted the thermometer and took a note of the reading. 'This man is not long deceased, probably alive less than twenty-four hours ago. Well, I have done all I need to do here. If you have taken all the photographs you want to take, we can have him removed to York District and I'll commence the post-mortem. Will you be observing for the police?'

'Yes, ma'am, Yellich's knocking on doors.'

'Any idea of his identity?' Dr D'Acre stood.

'Not yet, ma'am, but someone will report him missing. I am sure...Of that, I am very sure.'

Somerled Yellich 'got a result' at only the third door upon which he knocked. The house, like the other houses in the street, was a compact, semi-detached, owner-occupied house that he believed to have been built in the 1930s. In the main they were 'ribbon development' houses constructed along the arterial roads leading out of the towns and cities with occasional short offshoots, like branches from a tree. The houses of this type had small front gardens, a larger rear garden, and originally had a wooden garage for the family car at the top corner of the rear garden. These houses were held up by the modern historian as an illustration of the fact that the so-called 'hungry thirties' were only hungry in highly localized areas of heavy, traditional industry. Elsewhere in Britain, people enjoyed the prosperity of being able to afford to buy a house of the ilk that Yellich was calling on and were also able to afford a mass-produced car from Dagenham or Cowley to put in the garage. A few could even afford foreign holidays.

Yellich walked up to the yellow-painted front door of the house and rang the bell. He didn't hear it ring inside the building and so knocked on the door and caused a dog to bark. A few moments later a tall and very thinly built man opened the door. He seemed to Yellich to be in his late fifties. He looked quizzically at Yellich but didn't speak.

'Police.' Yellich held the pause before speaking. He showed his ID. Still the man didn't answer.

'Calling on houses to see if anyone saw anything. There was an incident in the woods last night.'

'An incident?' The man spoke with a strong, local accent but seemed to Yellich to be disinclined to give much of himself.

'A body was found. We suspect foul play.'

'Ah.' The man paused.

'Did you see anything, sir?'

'Aye...'

'You did?'

'Possibly.'

'What?'

'Motor car...white van.'

Yellich's heart missed a beat. 'Where? When?'

The man nodded. 'The other side of the wood. The wood has a couple of entrances for children to access it, and folk to walk their dogs. I don't like going into the woods by myself in case I am taken for something I'm not, but I like to get out of an evening... helps me sleep if I take a walk and there is pavement all round the wood. Only these houses overlook the wood, Greaves Wood, it's called, but turn left at my gate, brings you up to the main road. Walk along the main road and take the first left into Watch Lane, and Watch Lane curves round and joins this road. So I do that walk when I can, when the weather is dry. Takes me about an hour to get round...then I sleep well. The entrance to the wood, one of the entrances, is off Watch Lane.

'Was in two minds about doing it last night; it was dry but cold...but...I knew I'd sleep better if I did the walk, so put on my long johns and a pullover and my old duffel coat and went out...got quite warm after a while, so I walked down Watch Lane and saw a white van draw up outside the entrance to the wood, just a narrow path between houses, but it was dark, a few lights from the houses but not many street lamps and no street lamps at all anywhere near the entrance to Greaves Wood. I stopped walking and nudged into some shrubs...vans... cars...vehicles...they don't park there, not at night. It just looked suspicious.'

'Yes.' Yellich nodded his head slowly. 'I know what you mean.'

'You would do...as a copper. Anyway, I watched, and these two figures got out of the van. They went round the back, opened the door and took out this large bundle.'

'Bundle?'

'Well, it was wrapped in a sheet...or a carpet...took two of them to shift it...carried it into the woods. I stayed there, snuggled into the shrubs. It was very odd by then but not so odd as to have to call the police because Greaves Wood is used for fly-tipping, folks dump their old mattresses and televisions and wait for someone else to clear it up. The council has a blitz every now and again, so I thought fly-tippers, not a 999 call, and I don't have one of those pocket phones that young people carry to use to ruin the evening in the pub for everybody else. It would have taken me half an hour to get back home...so I just watched.'

'Understandable.'

'Anyway, the two people came back and eventually they drove off. Didn't see me.'

'Eventually?'

'Aye...the man was upset...he looked weak at the knees, staggered across the road, didn't want to get in the van...took his gloves off and held on to the front gate of the house opposite the entrance to Greaves Wood.'

'Took his gloves off?'

'Yes...why? Were you thinking of finger-prints? I watch crime dramas on TV.'

'Yes, I am. What time was this?'

'About eleven thirty.'

'That's less than twelve hours...they could still be there. Can you show me which gate?'

'Aye. Are we walking?'

'No, I'll have a car collect us.' He took out

his mobile phone. 'Two persons?' Yellich jabbed his phone. 'A man and...a woman? A boy?'

'A woman.'

'Age?'

'Well, adults...but younger rather than older.'

Yellich spoke when his call was answered and requested a car to pick him up. 'Did they speak?'

'Aye, the woman said, "Hurry up, you can be sick at home". That was when he was leaning on the gate looking like he was going to faint. She was in control alright...she drove the van.'

'You didn't hear a name, or anything?'

'No...posh, though.'

'Posh?'

'Aye...posh...no accent, talked like the newsreaders talk...English, but no accent other than an English accent. I'll get my coat.'

'Have you seen this?' Dr D'Acre handed Hennessey an early edition of the evening paper. 'I see you gave a press release.'

'We had to.' Hennessey leaned forward

and took the newspaper from Dr D'Acre. 'Wow...talk about lurid headlines: "The Cremators' Fourth Victim"? That will push up sales.'

'I imagine it will.' Dr D'Acre stood. 'Doubtless even the international press will be contacting you soon. No story moves newsprint like a serial killer. Well, shall we get on?'

'Yes, indeed.' Hennessey laid the paper on Dr D'Acre's desk in her small, cramped office and stood. 'I'll see you in there.'

'Difficult.' The Scenes of Crime Officer dusted the wooden gate. 'Exposure to the atmosphere never helps. Car thieves leave the windows of the car open to destroy any latents they might have left behind; that's if they don't torch the thing...which is what they did to mine.'

'Really?'

'Yes, really, Sergeant Yellich. My old VW ...just wannabe car thieves, learning the trade, no car thief worth his salt would steal an old, rusty VW, but these boys all have to learn an apprenticeship.' The SOCO stood back and picked up his camera with a flash attachment from behind his case and photographed the latents. 'Two hands,' he said. 'Palm prints on this side of the gate, fingerprints on the other. The man gripped the gate like this...' He made a motion of gripping the gate with both hands when standing with his back to the road. 'Gripped quite hard too.'

'That corresponds to what our witness said.'

'I'll ask the householders for their prints for the purposes of elimination, but who grips their own front gate like that? I mean, not many...not many in my book.'

'Nor in mine.' Yellich turned away from the gate. 'Nor in mine.'

'The deceased is an adult male,' Dr D'Acre spoke for the benefit of the microphone, 'extensively burned...'

It proceeded to be a very rapid post-mortem, for Dr Louise D'Acre said she knew what to look for. Having identified the deceased as being European in terms of ethnicity and being approximately five feet ten inches or one metre seventy-three centimetres tall, allowing for more shrinkage than usual, 'because fire tends to contract the human body', she then determined that because of the absence of carbon deposits in the trachea that the fire was post-mortem. She then peeled the skin from the skull, having made an incision around the circumference above the ears. 'Yes, it's always easy if you know what to look for...massive force trauma to the rear of the skull...something linear...an iron bar...not a hammer, with a focussed point but, as I said, a long, thin instrument, but an instrument of strength. He has a thick skull; it would have taken some force to inflict this injury...quite some force. It is one of the thickest skulls I have seen.'

'Didn't know skulls varied in thickness.' Hennessey stood against the wall of the pathology laboratory dressed in the requisite green paper coveralls, head, body and feet.

'Oh, yes.' Dr D'Acre turned in his direction. 'Of varied thickness, quite varied. There is a condition known as "eggshell skull" of extreme thinness. Folk don't know they have such a condition until they bump their head and cause a fracture, which

246

sometimes is fatal. Did a PM on a young boy once, one of the ones I remember. You were present, weren't you, Eric?'

'Yes.' Eric Filey, the portly and jovial mortuary attendant, who was similarly dressed to Hennessey, nodded grimly, as he held a thirty-five millimetre camera with a flash attachment. 'Yes, it was one of the ones you tend to remember.'

'Irate father smacked his son round the head...flat of his hand...all of us have been tempted to do it and many of us have done it...killed his son outright. Felt sorry for the father...he was distraught, loved his little boy...he was suicidal, but that boy had an eggshell skull. It was a skull of such thinness that any accident in the rough and tumble of childhood may have...nay, would likely have been fatal. I was able to say that to him...it helped him in his grief a little...well ...that is a long-winded answer.' She paused and considered the corpse which lay face up on the stainless steel table, one of four in the room. 'That is my conclusion, Chief Inspector...death from a massive blow to the skull ...burning was post-mortem. I'll fax my report to you as soon as possible.'

'Appreciated.'

'Do we know who it is?'

'Wilson Weston, is his name.' The man was agitated. 'He's my father. He's not at home. There's nowhere else he can go...nowhere he has to go. He's not wandered in the head.'

The constable tapped his pen on the missing persons report pad. 'If you'd wait a moment please, sir. We don't take mis. per. reports in respect of adults unless they have been missing for twenty-four hours but, in this case I think our CID officers might want to speak to you.'

'Why...?' The man's face drained of colour.

'If you'd take a seat, please, sir?' The constable went to the office behind the enquiry desk and picked up the phone and dialled a four figure internal number. 'Front desk here, sir,' he said when his call was answered. 'PC Banks. There's a member of the public here, wanting to make a mis. per. report...Less than twenty-four hours yet... Yes, sir, and adult, but the reason I am alerting you is that the description given fits that of the Code Four One of this morning, thought you might want to interview him? Yes...yes...thank you, sir.' PC Banks replaced the handset and walked back to the enquiry desk. 'Detective Sergeant Yellich will be out to see you, sir.'

'Thanks.' The man, sitting on the bench wringing his hands, nodded.

Moments later Yellich stepped into the public area and briefly spoke to PC Banks who pointed to the man sitting on the bench. Yellich approached him. 'Mr Weston?'

'Yes.' The man stood.

'Shall we talk in here?' Yellich opened the door of an interview room and Weston stepped in and sat down. Yellich sat opposite him.

'It's my father,' the man said with agitation.

'Whoa...' Yellich held up his hand. 'Let's take things one step at a time.'

'Sorry.' The man was thick set, wore an army surplus woollen pullover and denims, feet encased in solid, sensible winter boots. He rested a folded windcheater on his lap. His hands were fleshy with short, stubby fingers which were heavily nicotine stained.

'So you are?'

'John Weston, fifty years of age...unemployed...living on Alain Street, Tang Hall, number 127.

'I see.' Yellich wrote on his pad.

'And your father is missing?'

'Yes.'

'He is?'

'Wilson Weston...he's eighty...'

'Wilson?'

'Yes...it's a strange Christian name, it caused him problems all his life and he never forgave his parents for giving him that name, but there's always been a Wilson Weston as far back as we can trace and the curse fell on him...that's how he saw it anyway, as a curse.'

'I see.'

'That's why he called me John. I was the only boy of my generation so I escaped. Mind you, I wouldn't really have minded. John is such an ordinary name. I've often fancied a strange name...I might have amounted to something if I had had a strange name to grow into...'

Yellich smiled, 'Try Somerled.'

'Is that your name, sir?'

'Yes, spelled *s o m e r l e d*, pronounced "sorley"...It's Gaelic. Anyway, why do you believe your father is missing?'

'He's not at home. He lives alone...he's a widower...has a one-person flat on the Tang Hall estate as well, Allington Close, number 25. He is good for his age, he goes out for a walk each night. I don't mean evening...I mean night...to the end of Bad Bargain Lane and back, about half a mile. Not the full length of the lane but to where it crosses over the motorway...turns round and comes back, no matter what the weather. Except snow...can't walk in snow. So if there's thick snow he stays in, but always complains he feels the lack of "fresh".'

'Fresh?'

'Air...he likes a good lung full of fresh air each day...or night in his case. He's not at home this morning. I called round...I have a key. He didn't answer the door so I let myself in. I call on him every day, just to check on the old fella. He wasn't home, bed not slept in, mail on the floor not picked up, remains of the meal he'd had for supper in the kitchen sink, no sign of breakfast. He washes up each morning, you see, sir, that's his habit, his routine. Lets the dishes pile up in the sink then washes them all each morning after breakfast. Waits in for me to call each morning, then goes to the social club for lunch – it's a council run thing, does lunch for pensioners, ensures the old lads and lasses get at least one good meal each day of the week. Not open weekends. But today's...what? Thursday, so he would have waited in for me. His mind is as sharp as a tack. So I walked along the lane...not there. Mind, if he had been lying there after a heart attack or a stroke, somebody would have found him by the time I got there, but I had to do it.'

'Yes.'

'No trace of him. Phoned the hospitals... no one admitted...but you are seeing me?'

'Yes...there's no easy way to say this, so I'll just say it...a gentleman was murdered in the night, his body was found this morning. My boss is at the post-mortem now.'

'Post-mortem?'

'Yes.'

'Well, is it my father? If I could see him...I could identify him.'

'Well, that won't be possible, the body was damaged.'

'Oh.' John Weston sat back in his chair. 'You're not telling me...these...Cremators? I read the paper...no...no, not my dad?'

'We haven't identified the body.'

'Oh...no...no...no!' Weston buried his head in his hands. When he had sufficiently recovered, Yellich asked him if he had anything that could provide a DNA profile of Wilson Weston.

'What sort of thing are you looking for?'

'A hair from his scalp...that would be ideal.'

'Where could...?'

'A comb, hairbrush...bed sheets.'

'I'll look.'

'No...could you take me to your father's home?'

'Yes.'

'Did your father have any enemies?'

'Who would want to murder him?'

'Yes.'

'No...in fact he was a very quietly living man since my mother died...that was fifteen years ago. Moved into Tang Hall then, took his single person's flat...seems to be on nodding terms with most folk but not close to anyone. He's not the sort of bloke to rub folk up the wrong way.'

'Alright.' Yellich stood. 'I'll bring my car round to the front of the building. If you'd wait in the reception area?'

'It's not funny, George.' Commander Sharkey dropped the newspaper on Hennessey's desk. 'In fact, it's damned unfunny.'

'Yes, sir.'

'The "Cremators" indeed.' Sharkey sat in the chair in front of Hennessey's desk. 'So what progress have we made?'

We...we... Hennessey thought, there was not a great deal of 'we' in it that might include Commander Sharkey. 'Well, we have made some progress...and in fairness, sir, it is still early days.'

'Four victims is not early days, George, these are serial killers.'

'Yes, sir, but with respect, this investigation is still only six days old.'

'It is four victims old, George, that's how old it is. So, what progress?'

'We have descriptions of the perpetrators and their likely vehicle, which will have been dumped by now or re-sprayed.'

'Yes.'

'Well...that's about it, sir. We allowed ourselves to get sidetracked a bit with the first two murders, the husband and wife, which was a double murder, a single incident, so the four victims represent only three crimes ...but in the case of the first two there did at least seem to be motivation and a likely suspect, although it now appears that we were wrong.'

'Wrong?' Sharkey sighed.

'There was still only one crime at that point!' Hennessey allowed an edge to creep into his voice. He often heard his pension calling his name but never more earnestly or loudly than when he was with the officious commander who, senior in rank, was ten or fifteen years his junior.

'Very well. What's your next move?'

'A consultation with Dr Joseph at the university since you have obtained approval for the funding.'

'When?'

Hennessey glanced at his watch. 'Well...I should be leaving now, sir, if I am to be courteous and arrive on time.'

'Very well.' Sharkey stood and allowed himself a glance out of the small window of Hennessey's office. 'Tourists, in this weather?'

Hennessey followed his gaze and saw a small group of elderly people who wore brightly coloured clothing, much more brightly coloured than any Briton would wear walking the walls. Probably Americans, he thought. 'Well, don't need heat and sun to enjoy ancient buildings or ghost walks, sir, and it brings in the money from year end to year end...not just for a few months each summer.'

'Dare say. Well, we must be courteous and so I'll let you get on...but I want daily progress reports.'

'Yes, sir.'

Hennessey had in fact a full ninety minutes before the appointed time of his consultation with Dr Joseph but he had seized the opportunity to rid himself of Sharkey's company. He had intended to drive the short distance from Micklegate Bar to the university campus at Heslington but, having freed himself from the commander's clutches upon a subterfuge, he needed to then vacate the building and, disliking driving even short distances, for reasons of which the gracious reader is already acquainted, he resolved to walk. The walk would in fact be quite pleasant, he decided, wrapped up against the wind with hat and scarf and overcoat, woollen trousers and good, comfortable and above all, dry footwear; it would indeed be very pleasant. A walk is good for freeing up the mind. For George Hennessey there had been times in his career that breakthroughs had been made towards the end of a sixty-minute stroll. For him a sixty-minute stroll problem was the equivalent of Sherlock Holmes' 'two pipe problems'.

Having signed out, he left the red brick Victorian building at Micklegate Bar, followed the walls of the ancient city to Ballie Hill. Again he enjoyed that particular stretch of wall which was always relatively free of other foot passengers, and which offered a delightful prospect to the north of proud and neatly kept terraced houses 'within the walls', and to the south, of the rooftops of the city and ending with a few paces through a small copse which he always found enchanting. He crossed the flat and deceptively peaceful looking Ouse at Skeldergate Bridge and with some difficulty avoiding traffic, crossed into Tower Street and entered Fishergate. From Fishergate he walked into Kent Street of smaller terraced houses, which being without the walls, lacked the prestige and the value of similar properties within the walls, and from there walked on to Heslington Lane, past The Retreat operated by the Quakers and then appropriately or inappropriately, he thought, depending on one's point of view, entered Thief Lane of pleasant suburban houses which offered a view of the university buildings across the fields to his right. He turned gratefully into University Road and escaped the wind which had been blowing keenly into his face since he left Fishergate, and entered the grounds of the campus.

He enjoyed the walk within the grounds of the university, its square, modern construction, its angular clock tower, the lake on which were wildfowl, and noted few persons about, the institution by then being 'down' for Christmas. He stepped out of the chill wind into the warmth of a low-rise, centrally heated building and climbed a set of stairs to the first floor. He walked along the corridor until he came to a polished pinewood door on which was the nameplate 'Kamilla Joseph PhD'. He took off his hat, unwound his scarf, unbuttoned his overcoat and tapped softly on the door but could not resist using the well-honed knock of the police officer, tap, tap...tap.

'Come in.' The reply was prompt and reverential and warm. No imperious 'Come' after an equally imperious wait. Here was humility and, thought Hennessey, all the more humble since the expertise of Dr Joseph was of worldwide renown within the field of forensic psychology.

Hennessey entered the office. Dr Joseph smiled warmly at him and stood and extended her hand. 'We meet again, Chief Inspector.'

'Indeed.' Hennessey shook her hand. He found her grip to be strong, though not over strong, which pleased him. He so detested those who give a 'wet lettuce' handshake with no grip at all.

'Please.' She indicated the chair in front of

her desk with a sweep of an open palm and she too sat.

Hennessey noticed a neatly kept office, plants of a low maintenance variety, money plants, spider plants and cacti on the windowsill and also on her desk. Behind her on the wall was pinned an airline poster advertising Dr Joseph's native Brunei.

'Well...' She opened the file. 'I've not had a proper chance to study your report.'

'Yes. Very short notice...sorry.'

'No matter, I did what I could. Well, the terms "organized" and "disorganized" killer are now old hat but they still offer a useful starting point. So, there are now four victims, I understand? There's just three in the file.'

'Yes, Doctor...the fourth victim seems to us to fit the pattern...elderly...'

'Yes.'

'No known enemies according to his son who was interviewed by DS Yellich earlier today.'

'Alright.'

'No one would appear to benefit from his death; he was not a wealthy man.'

'Alright.'

'The gentleman was clubbed over the head, then by some means taken to a place we have yet to find, where his body was burned...definitely deceased when he was set alight.'

'Thankfully.'

'Indeed.'

'Then dumped in woodland.'

'So...attempt to conceal the identity by burning the corpse and once burned, it's discarded in a not particularly remote place?'

'Yes, that appears to be the case.'

'Incinerated to hide identity...a bit fatuous.'

'Yes. It didn't take us long to establish identity in all four cases.'

'So the perpetrators know little of scientific developments?'

'It would seem so.'

'Unlearned, perhaps?' Kamy Joseph raised her eyebrow.

'Perhaps.'

'Well, you see the problem I have with this dossier is accepting that the victims fit a profile. They are middle aged/elderly white persons, but beyond that there is more dissimilarity between the first two victims, Mr and Mrs Dent, and the second two. The first two are significantly more youthful than the second two victims, the first two were related, husband and wife, the second two are unrelated.'

'Yes...we can find no contact between the third and fourth victim.'

'The first two were professionally employed, wealthy and would be difficult to approach as a stranger...'

'Yes.'

'The second two were not at all wealthy and would be easier to approach, possibly less wary of being mugged. Was the fourth victim also attacked whilst walking in a remote place...alone?'

'Yes, he was...late at night on Bad Bargain Lane, edge of the city, fields either side.'

'You see, that strengthens my argument; I do not see a clear victim profile.'

'Not two independent teams of killers acting contemporaneously with each other?' Hennessey's hand went to his forehead. 'That would be too much.'

'No,' Kamy Joseph said as she held up her hand, 'don't jump the gun, Chief Inspector, don't rush your fences...just bear with me.' She paused. 'There are aspects of the case which also don't add up. The first two victims...husband and wife, very difficult to attack two persons as a stranger, so the first crime would seem to have some forward thinking, some planning to it. The weapon was absent at the scene and the victims' bodies were transported. Those are characteristics of an organized killer but such killers do not know their victims. The first two victims, Mr and Mrs Dent, could only have been approached by someone whom they knew. Some previous knowledge of the victim is a characteristic of a disorganized killer, as was once the term, as is the fact that the crime scene was random and careless, and the body in each case was left in the open, partially hidden, but not buried or dismembered and scattered. Also, in the case of a disorganized killer, we would expect the weapon to be at the scene or carelessly discarded, which it wasn't. That is one of the reasons why forensic psychology has moved on from classifying killers as organized and disorganized...it just isn't that neat, just isn't so clear-cut, but here...'

She patted the file. 'Here something else is going on. In all cases there is a primary crime scene, a secondary crime scene and disposal site…a tertiary crime scene. That is consistent. That is a clear indication that we are looking for the same two killers in each case.'

'Thank goodness for that.'

'And the crimes occurred at night?'

'Yes.'

'More commonality…?'

'Again, yes.'

'As is the attempt to protect the identity of the killers, and their successful escape.'

Hennessey sat forward.

'I can also tell you that the perpetrators of these crimes are local. They live in York or near York. They are marauders, striking out of a base and attacking locally…so it would seem to me. I feel that because of the very short time window from the first two to the fourth and thus far final victim. A commuter, one who travels from his home some distance away would not attack as frequently, and their victims would also be more spread out, geographically speaking. The commuter would leave victims along the A1 from London to Edinburgh, for example.'

'I see.'

'Someone is in a hurry here, and not in a hurry to kill as many elderly people as possible.' She sat back in her chair. 'Something else is happening here.'

'What do you suggest?'

'Well...someone is at pains to convince you as rapidly as they can that you do in fact have a serial killer on your hands...which in fact you do, but not the randomly targeting killer he or they want you to think.'

'Camouflage killing?'

'That would be my guess, reading this file. I have read of such, but never come across one.'

'It's a new one for me as well.' Hennessey ran his liver-spotted hand through his silver hair. 'We are talking about the same thing here? Wherein a series of murders occur... they seem random...'

'Yes.'

'But one of the murders...just one, has a personal motive?'

'Yes, that's what I am thinking.'

'The others are random...the police think serial killer?'

265

'That's it.'

'And so the one person who has the motive to kill one specific victim is not a suspect?'

'Yes, so who would want you to rapidly eliminate him or them from your list of suspects?'

'Fellow called Gregory Dent.' Hennessey clenched his fist and brought it down on the arm of the chair. 'Damn him. It's all so clear now.'

'Better bring him in before another elderly person meets his maker marginally earlier than he would otherwise do.'

Yellich drove home to Huntingdon and parked his car outside his modest new-build house on the estate. He walked up the drive as the door opened and Jeremy ran out of the house to greet his father. Yellich stopped and braced himself for the impact just as Jeremy crashed against him with an arm-enveloping, head-burying hug of warmth and affection. Together they walked into the house and into the kitchen where Sara was preparing the evening meal. Yellich embraced his wife, and after eliciting the intelligence that Jeremy had been 'very good' since he was returned from school, Yellich, in keeping with established practice, changed into more casual clothing and took Jeremy for a walk. They walked into the old village and then to the playing fields by the parish church and to the stream, identifying plants and birds as they saw them. It had been hard for Somerled and Sara Yellich when they were told that their son would never be 'normal' and the sense of disappointment was profound, but great joy had come unexpectedly. That sense of childish wonder never left their son, that warmth, that faith in his parents. They also met parents of other children with learning difficulties who offered mutual support and from which grew valued friendships. It was, they had found, like a previously hitherto unknown world opening up for them. With affection and stimulation Jeremy, they were advised, could develop a mental age of twelve by the time he was in his early twenties and be able to live a semi-independent life in a supervised hostel.

Later, with Jeremy upstairs and sleeping the sleep of the just, Sara and Somerled

Yellich sat together on the settee relaxing with a glass of wine each.

'And to think,' she said, 'to think, I would have been Head of English in a comprehensive school by now if you had not dragged me off to the institution called marriage, intelligent females for the disposal of.'

'Would you turn the clock back if you could?'

'Nope...' She nestled her head into his chest. 'Wouldn't turn it back at all...not for one second.'

In the large kitchen of a solid half-timbered house in Skelton a man and a woman sat in silence with an empty teapot sitting on the table, as teenage and pre-teenage feet ran backwards and forwards until silence once again descended on the home. They talked softly and when, after thirty minutes had elapsed and no further sound had come from upstairs, Louise D'Acre smiled and said, 'Well, they're settled. Shall we go up now?'

'Yes,' George Hennessey said as he returned the smile. 'Yes...let's go up.'

It was Thursday, 22.47 hours.

Eight

Friday, December 19, 9.35 hours –
*in which a jury deliberates and a middle-aged
couple enjoy a cliff top stroll.*

The twin cassettes of the tape recorder spun
slowly, the red recording light glowed softly.

'The time is 9.35 hours, on Friday the
nineteenth of December; the place is Interview Room Two in Micklegate Bar Police
Station, York. I am Detective Chief Inspector Hennessey. I am now going to ask the
other persons present to identify themselves.'

'Detective Sergeant Yellich.'

'Ambrose Peebles. Ellis, Burden, Wood-
land and Lake, solicitors, representing Mr
Dent under the terms of the Police and
Criminal Evidence Act 1985.'

'Gregory Dent.' He smiled and, thought Hennessey, he looked very confident, too damned confident, once again that cat-got-the-cream sort of confidence, trick-up-his-sleeve sort of confidence.

'Mr Dent, you have been arrested in connection with the murder of your parents—'

'Adoptive parents,' Dent interrupted Hennessey, 'adoptive parents.'

'Alright...with the murder of your adoptive parents Anthony and Muriel Dent of West End House, Great Sheldwich, and you have been cautioned. Is that correct?'

'Yes.' Dent nodded. 'Though I prefer the old caution...the new one just doesn't have the poetry, somehow.'

'Let's stay with the issue,' Hennessey growled.

'OK.' Dent smiled.

Ambrose Peebles, portly, expensive suit, bespectacled, glanced at Dent with clear irritation.

'You murdered your parents for a motive as yet unknown, but probably greed. They were very wealthy.'

'Yes...they were. And now I am also wealthy.' He held eye contact with Hennessey. 'I inherited half their estate, the other half went to my sister.'

'So you had motive?'

'Yes.'

'You agree?'

'Of course, twelve million motives, though I confess I didn't know they were that wealthy.'

'Twelve million!'

'The estate, over all, has been valued at approximately twenty-four million. They were in possession of a large tract of prime building land, in the centre of the city, and had acquired other similar plots in neighbouring towns. It has to be liquidized yet... so I am jumping the gun when I say that I am also wealthy...but a matter of weeks, really.'

'Killing for money is as old...' Hennessey faltered. 'It's...well, it's old, we come across it time and time again, but why the other two? What harm...?' Hennessey paused as he felt his anger rising. 'You see, it fell apart ...it just didn't look like a serial killer, despite what the papers called you.'

' "The Cremators"? Yes, I read that.'

'It fell apart very rapidly. You made a

number of errors...our forensic psychologist saw through them. You might have fooled the press but you didn't fool a psychologist.'

'What errors?'

Hennessey eyed Dent keenly. 'Am I hearing a confession?'

'Nope.' Dent smiled. 'But I am curious about the errors.'

'Why?'

'General interest...I am quite close to this case...I lost my adoptive parents, I am accused of their murder, I have a right to be interested. You would be interested too, if you were sitting here.'

'Well, I am not sitting there. You tried to pass off all four murders as the work of a serial killer.'

'Killers.' Dent relaxed in the chair. 'The newspapers spoke of a couple. "A murderous duo" I think they said...lurid...'

'Yes...you and Miss Thurnham.'

'Mrs Thurnham...she is not yet divorced.'

'Mrs Thurnham, we'll be talking to her next.'

'OK.'

'One of you will crack.'

'We will?'

'One of you...we will find evidence to link you to one of the murders.'

'You will?'

'Please, Mr Hennessey.' Peebles glanced at Hennessey over the rim of his spectacles. 'Please ask questions. This is not the time or place for threats.'

Hennessey nodded. 'Very well, did you murder Mr and Mrs Dent and two other elderly persons, namely—'

'No...no...no...no...no...and...no.' Dent's voice was calm, steady, unfaltering. 'No...I did not murder anyone.'

'We have only to find the white van.'

'If it's white...if it were mine, I would have re-sprayed it or burned it out. I would have reported it stolen...and by burning it, I would remove any evidence.'

'You hope so.'

'Well, I am after all allegedly...I repeat, allegedly, a cremator...an arsonist...a fire raiser...a fire setter...so I reckon I would set the van alight and burn any evidence that would link me to one of the murders...if I was the murderer...if I was one of them.'

Hennessey reached for the off switch. 'This interview is concluded at 9.47 hours.'

He switched off the machine and the red light dimmed and then vanished.

'So I am free to go?'

'No, we have twelve hours from the moment of arrest to decide whether to charge you. Please stay here.' Hennessey turned to the solicitor. 'Will you be accompanying us, Mr Peebles, or do we need a separate solicitor for Mrs Thurnham?'

'I can observe under the terms of the Police and Criminal Evidence Act...but if charges are brought, each defendant will then need a separate solicitor.'

'Thank you.'

Susan Thurnham, smartly dressed, sat impassively as Hennessey switched on the recorder and then invited all present to identify themselves for the tape. He then said, 'You know why you have been arrested, Mrs Thurnham?'

'Please make it a question...a clear question,' Ambrose Peebles spoke softly. 'PACE rules require such. A tape recorder can't hear a question mark.'

'Very well. Do you know why you have been arrested, Mrs Thurnham?'

'Yes.' She clearly wasn't giving anything away.

'And you have been cautioned? Sorry... sorry,' Hennessey held up his hand before Ambrose Peebles could object, 'and is it true that you have been cautioned?'

'Yes.'

'What do you know of the murders of Mr and Mrs Anthony and Muriel Dent?'

'Oh...they were first killed, then set on fire after they were dead...at a place still unknown.' She brushed her hair back.

Hennessey had to concede that she did look quite fetching in her working clothes: pinstriped jacket and skirt, dark nylons and black shoes.

She continued, 'Then their bodies were dumped beside the river where they were found...that was about a week ago, yes...a week today in fact.'

'All of which was reported in the press.'

'Yes...which is all that I know.'

Hennessey paused. 'We know that this was a clumsy attempt to make the murders look like the work of a serial killer. Mr and Mrs Dent were murdered for a motive, two other elderly persons were murdered at random.

We know that a couple was involved, a man and a woman who spoke with received pronunciation.'

'Oh yes, that was reported...I forgot that.'

'And you and Mr Gregory Dent can only alibi each other.'

'Well, that is an alibi...why are you wasting your time? Why are you wasting my time?'

'Because I believe that you and Gregory Dent murdered all four persons for the purpose of inheriting the Dents' fortune.'

'Well, all you have to do is to prove it. But I can tell you that you will not do so.'

'We won't?'

'No...you won't. There is no evidence to link us to the murders because we did not commit them.'

There was a warmth in her eyes, Hennessey had seen the look before. 'You are going to tell us something?'

'Yes...well, probably, I don't know for certain. I don't want to do your job for you, but sitting here it did focus my mind...but it occurs to me that someone else benefits from the death of Mr and Mrs Dent.'

'Their adoptive daughter?' Hennessey's jaw sagged.

'Well...doesn't she? And she is in a relationship...her husband...both speak with received pronunciation, a few short northern vowels but nearer to RP than accented English and he, well, I understand that he drives to and from his job at the training college in...'

'A white van?'

'Well...it was white when I last saw it.' She smiled. 'So gentle a couple...so warm...the last person or persons you would think of being capable of multiple murder...but then I dare say, so was Jack the Ripper. Talk to the Vicarys.'

In the event it was Leonard Vicary who broke first. He cracked very easily. Whereas Juliette Vicary, bereaved early in life, a period in a children's home, then adoptive care, she had something of the ghetto about her, so Hennessey thought, more like her brother. But Leonard, a mild-mannered college lecturer, had never been in trouble with the police before. All Hennessey had to do was to leave him in an interview room for an hour or two, and when he returned, after being unable to extract a confession from

Juliette Vicary, it was to find the man trembling with emotion, desperately holding back tears.

'So whose idea was it?' he asked gently, the tape recorder being switched on, all present having identified themselves again, and the place and time having been established.

'Gregory's...who else?'

'So, what was the plan?'

'To make it look like a serial killer was on the loose. Gregory said that he and Susan...'

'She was part of this?'

'Oh yes...very enthusiastic. Gregory said that he would invite suspicion, that would mean we would not be suspected, and because Gregory and Susan hadn't done the crimes, nothing could be proved, the case would go cold.'

'It would take a very long time for four murders to go cold, Mr Vicary, a very long time.'

'It sounded so simple. They made it sound so simple.'

'And the motive...money?'

'Yes, you've seen our house. It might look comfortable but we are struggling...a junior lecturer's salary is...low...and the Dents live a long time, that family make very old bones. Anthony Dent's father might still be alive now if he hadn't stepped in front of a motorbike. We'd have reached retirement before we inherited anything, and as Gregory and Juliette said, they were not their parents, anyway.'

'And you went along with that? So much for their money being kept in a trust fund for children not yet born.'

'Yes.' He pressed his hands to his eyes. 'Yes, Gregory, he has this way of making people do things...and Juliette...she's very pushy. Once we had killed the Dents we had to go through with the rest of the plan, no going back.'

'Who killed the Dents?'

Leonard Vicary shrugged. 'I did...banged them on the head with a golf club.'

'Where?'

'In our living room. We pretended to bump into them when they had had their evening meal and we invited them back to our house. Made sure of them by putting their heads in plastic bags. Carried them out, put them in the van, took them out into the country...doused with petrol...put the flames out before they went out, then brought the bodies back into the city and left them where they'd be found.'

'Why burn the bodies?'

'Gregory's idea. He said all serial killers have hallmarks, so we burned all the bodies ...not totally incinerated them, just wanted a hallmark and a fire attracts attention, didn't want to let them burn too long...I've ruined my life.'

'Yes.' Hennessey remained softly spoken. 'Yes, you have...but a full confession...a guilty plea...statements implicating Gregory Dent and Susan Thurnham...play your cards right in prison, you might breath free air while you are still young enough to appreciate it.'

'Yes...everything you want.' He sat back. 'I feel better for telling you...I couldn't have lived with myself. So, where did we go wrong? What was the slip up that led you to us? I have to know...'

'You didn't slip up. You were not even under suspicion at all until Susan Thurnham suggested we chat to you.'

Leonard Vicary's face paled, he grabbed the edge of the table, his jaw set firm. 'She fed us to you...they fed us to you...all along...all along...that was their plan.'

Hennessey too felt a certain impact in the pit of his stomach. He knew Vicary was correct. He saw it...he saw it all now. So calculating, so mercilessly evil...but proving it...proving it...that was going to be the obstacle.

Due to the defendants inviting considerable local hostility, it was requested by the defence, and not opposed by the Crown, that the trial be moved to another location where an impartial jury could be empanelled. Consequently, six months after their arrest, Regina versus Vicary, Vicary, Dent and Thurnham took place, in the middle of a heat-wave, at Newcastle Crown Court. Leonard and Juliette Vicary pleaded guilty to four charges of murder and each collected four life sentences, to be served concurrently, the judge recommending parole be considered only after each defendant had served a minimum of twenty years imprisonment. Gregory Dent and Susan Thurnham pleaded not guilty to conspiracy to murder.

The white-wigged, black-gowned lawyer for the Crown invited the jury to consider the cold and calculated manner 'which defies belief' by which the accused persuaded the Vicarys to commit not one, but four acts of murder, and then informed on them, 'like feeding them to the lions', so that Gregory Dent would acquire his sister's share of their inheritance, the law not permitting anyone to profit from crime. In the event of Juliette Vicary's guilt being established, her inheritance would automatically pass to her brother, Gregory Dent, there being no codicil in the will to allow Mr Anthony Dent's brother or any other relative at all to inherit anything of the estate of Anthony and Muriel Dent. 'The law of inheritance being quite clear...it is like a cross, it goes up and down before it goes from side to side,' he explained. 'In the absence of a will, parents and children inherit before brothers or sisters.'

'Not so,' said the equally bewigged and be-gowned counsel for the defence. 'It is, as my learned friend for the prosecution has himself stated in his own words, it is quite beyond belief that a man should manipulate his own sister into committing these crimes so that she would be disinherited, thus allowing him to inherit her fortune. Quite beyond belief. What is happening here, ladies and gentlemen of the jury, is that this is nothing more than a malicious attempt by the Vicarys to implicate Gregory Dent and Susan Thurnham in their crime, so as to soften the blow by dragging my clients down with them. It is nothing more than that. Further, a conviction for an offence of this magnitude requires proof, if it is to be a safe conviction. Proceeding on the balance of probability is simply not allowed...there must be proof, and there is no proof. There is no independent witness to the conspiracy being planned. It is but the word of two convicted murderers against the word of two people of good character. For that reason and that reason alone, a conviction would be wholly unsafe and I urge you to acquit both defendants.'

The jury retired and after three days of deliberation returned a majority verdict of Not Guilty in respect of both Gregory Dent and Susan Thurnham.

★ ★ ★

The middle-aged man and the younger, but only slightly younger, woman, strolled arm in arm along the cliff path enjoying the warmth of the evening.

'Those are his caravans,' said the man, 'see in the distance, little white boxes in the field?'

'Oh, really...?'

'Or they were his...he's sold them...he's liquidizing it all, they're moving south with their millions.'

'So unfair...setting up his sister like that, and her husband...and getting away with it.'

'Yes.' It was all the man felt he could say. 'Well,' he said after a pause, 'back to the hotel, a meal and an early night...would you like that?'

'Yes.' Louise D'Acre turned and smiled at George Hennessey. 'Yes, I would like that very much...very much indeed.'